SUMMER CRUSH

SUMMER CRUSH

THE TOURNAMENT: VOLUME FOUR

_____

B. B. GRIFFITH

GRIFFITH PUBLISHING

DENVER

Griffith Publishing
Denver

Publication Information

Summer Crush (The Tournament, #4)

ISBN: 978–0–9899400–7–8

Copyright: Griffith Publishing LLC ©2014

First published 2014

Written by B. B. Griffith

Enquiries should be made to the publisher:

info@griffithpublishing.com

Publisher Information

Griffith Publishing LLC is a registered trademark.

For more information about the Tournament visit online at www.griffithpublishing.com

To Lee Z.

Welcome to the family.

I feel like a ghost wandering in a world grown alien.
I cannot cast out the old way of writing, and I cannot
acquire the new. I have made an intense effort to feel the
musical manner of today, but it will not come to me.

—Sergei Rachmaninoff

CHAPTER ONE

GREER NICHOLS FOUND a rose on his front doormat when he went out to get his morning paper. He actually stepped right over it at first, but when he grabbed the *San Francisco Chronicle* from his front lawn and turned to go back inside, he saw it: a single–stemmed yellow rose.

Greer paused. He didn't receive roses. Greer was an administrator, not a player. Very few people knew where he lived, and none of them were romantics. He tucked his silk robe tighter around his boxy frame and spun slowly. Nobody in sight. He ran one hand over his gleaming head, smooth and black as an eight ball. When he brought it away, he realized he was shaking, and his fingertips were damp. It seemed his body had put two and two together before his brain could. This was no admirer's token but rather the calling card he'd heard whispers of. This was an ultimatum. Greer took another look at the thick ring of redwood trees that bordered his house. He looked at his sedan: five hundred horsepower coated in early morning California dew. He wished for one moment that he could hop in that car and rip through those trees and never look back. But it was too late for that.

You didn't run from the rose.

From what he'd heard, you *couldn't* run from the rose.

Greer set his jaw, dropped his paper back on the lawn, and walked back in the house, crushing the rose underfoot as he went. He had some work to do before they came for him. He locked the door behind him and moved straight to his office, a half–moon room set in the back of the house with windows open to the sweeping forest and the city beyond. He sat behind his desk, reached over to his computer, and flipped open a thumb-print pad on the side of the box. His monitor blinked on.

Total wipe? read the prompt. A cursor blinked below.

Greer typed *yes*.

Password?

Without hesitation, Greer typed in a twenty–four–character sequence.

Step Away.

Greer pushed his rolling chair back, and a searing hiss emanated from his hard drive. There was a brief, flash–paper brightness and then the acrid tang of burning metal. The monitor flashed once and then went permanently black. *That was the easy part*, Greer thought. He pushed his chair over to a large cabinet on the far wall. He powered up a shredder and began pulling with his left hand and shredding documents with his right.

After a time, he paused, sweating, and turned the shredder off. It wound down with a sad whine, and Greer listened to the silence. It was strange that he'd had this much time. It was as if they didn't care what he destroyed, as if they didn't care what he knew or what he had.

Greer Nichols knew he was going to die.

And in that moment, he didn't weep or scream or run. His mind didn't go blank with terror. In fact, the first thought that came to him was *I'm really glad I didn't waste my time re–doing the house.* The thought made him laugh with a force that startled him.

He reached under the left side of the cabinet where the foot wasn't flush with the wooden floor and pressed a small button. A hidden weight dropped inside the shelving with a heavy *thunk*, and a small panel kicked out. Greer pulled it open with his fingernails. He looked at the small packet of folders within and contemplated shredding them too. But he didn't. He closed the panel with a soft click.

For many years, Greer had kept just one picture on his desk: a poorly framed shot of three people bunched under an awning out of the rain, laughing at the storm. They were Johnnie Northern, Max Haulden, and Nikkie Hix. The first generation of Team Blue—his team—before their fall. They looked young, more like kids waiting to get back out on the sports field than warriors. Even after their demise, he'd kept the picture. Whatever history might think of them, Greer knew that at one time, at least, they were friends. But about ten years ago, he'd swapped that picture out. The one sitting there now was a shot of the second generation of Team Blue, not the official team shot that they handed out at autograph sessions, but another shot from the same sitting that captured a moment in time when all three had cracked up from holding a menacing stance for so long. It was a perfect moment: all three of them, Ellie Willmore, Cy Bell, and Tom Elrey with their heads thrown back and their mouths wide and toothy with laughter. Ellie had written a message to him on the bottom of the picture, mostly tongue in cheek:

Watch our backs!

Reading it, Greer sank back into his chair for the first time that morning. He became very aware of his creaky hands and his aching neck. He thought he'd been old when he took this job running Blue's front office and serving as the only real connection the three players had to the massive organization that was the Tournament. He hadn't been old then. Thirty–eight wasn't old. *Thirty–eight is the batter's box.* That was twenty years ago. Gone in a blink. *It's a shame,* Greer thought. *Body withstanding, I feel younger now than I did then.*

For the tenth time, he thought about calling Ellie. He had that privilege. He could call any of them if he wanted. But what would he say? There was nothing they could do. He was proud as hell of all three of them, but they knew that. He was so damn proud that, in ten years, he'd never been able to figure out how to say it, but they knew. If he tried to pack it into one last call from the deck of the Titanic, he'd just confuse and scare everyone. He couldn't even rightly say who was coming for him.

Still, he felt lonely now. With nothing else to shred, Greer's mind finally caught up. His fate settled on his shoulders. He wanted to hear Ellie's voice one last time. She was the closest he'd ever had to a daughter. He picked up his phone, but just then he heard a car pull up. He froze then gently set the phone back down. He thought about changing into one of his dozens of tailored suits—he preferred pinstripes. *Fuck it. I'll go out in a robe.*

He slid a revolver from his desk drawer into his grasp and spun in his chair to face the door. *As a matter of fact, I might just take this rose bastard with me.*

He expected them to break the door down. They didn't. They had a key. He expected thugs to waltz in, but there were none. The door swung harmlessly open to reveal the California sunrise through the trees, nothing more.

Then someone bashed Greer in the back of the head, and his world went black.

*

Greer dreamed he was playing poker. The table was massive, hundreds of feet long and stretching into the distance. Spaced along it were the administrators of the Tournament teams. They laughed and bantered among themselves as they bet and checked and raised. But instead of chips, they splashed the pot with yellow rose petals, thousands and thousands of them, in a mound that reached into the sky. Greer tried to read the hand he was dealt, but the cards were blurry, and they seemed to vibrate in concert with the deeper pounding in his head. He woke in the back seat of a town car.

He shot to a sitting position and then reeled, holding himself steady against the window. A man sitting next to him eyed him carefully. A second man, similar in cut and make, drove the car. Greer recognized them. They were the Tournament equivalent of G–men, security officers in off–the–rack dark blue suits, interchangeable haircuts, and single–toned ties. Faces like theirs would be instantly forgotten. He'd called on these men once to bring in a man named Frank Youngsmith—a man he now counted as a close friend. They'd done their job and faded into the scenery.

A third man, sitting on the passenger's side, seemed different. He was young, with a boyish, smooth face. When he turned to regard Greer, Greer saw that the man was older than he looked, perhaps in his late thirties. He smiled at Greer, and it was pleasant in a distant–neighbor sort of way. His hair was an un–styled clump of soft brown. He wore a long–sleeved polo shirt with a rugby stripe and khaki shorts with running shoes. He had one leg up and crossed lightly over his other leg. His knee rested against the door handle.

"Hello Greer. Welcome back to us."

Greer didn't speak. Instead, he watched the road. They were cruising a barren strip of eastern California past flattened desert and endless telephone poles. They passed fast food joints and strip malls in the sad sort of decline Greer associated with the drive toward Las Vegas, well before any of the flashing lights and life of the Strip. He wondered how long he'd been out. He wondered if he'd been drugged.

"We're on Five–Eighty East, just past Livermore. In case you're wondering." The man bobbed his free foot up and down. "There's a really good Dairy Queen coming up here on your right. Clean bathrooms."

"Where are you taking me?" Greer cleared his throat.

"Middle of the desert."

"You're gonna kill me."

"I think so. Yes. I mean, I'm going to give you a choice, but I'm almost one hundred percent positive that you'll turn me down. Then I will kill you. Yes." He nodded, foot still bobbing. He pulled up his gray athletic sock.

"Who are you?" Greer asked.

"I'm the Gardner. I gave you the rose. Sort of a 'courting you' type of thing. It works. Most of the time. But like I said, with you?" He made a twirling motion with his index finger near his temple then turned it into a gun and mimed blowing his brains out.

Greer sat in silence during the rest of the ride. Nobody seemed to mind. Occasionally, the Gardner would point out frivolous roadside attractions, things like the world's largest rubber band ball or a ranch that birthed two five–legged cows, one after the other. All the while, the man to Greer's right stared intently at Greer's hands. Greer wondered if a sneeze might get him a fist to the temple.

When the car turned from the highway off onto a two–lane road leading south toward the foothills, the Gardner sat back and rocked in his seat with a benign smile. "Almost there, now."

Greer tried to place him. He tried with everything he had. He racked his brain to match the face, the voice, but he had nothing. He'd never seen this man before. And yet it appeared the Gardner had at least some authority over the Tournament's security wing. That must mean he was an insider. A bettor, perhaps? One of the influential oddsmakers?

At a tattered billboard, the town car cut left then rolled onto a dirt road for what Greer judged to be nearly two miles. They turned from the dirt road onto plain dirt. Flat desert. The car wove between rocks and cacti until they parked. In desert country, sound traveled, and Greer heard truckers downshifting in the distance, driving down a road many miles in the distance that he knew he'd never see again.

The Gardner was the first out. He stopped by the door and stretched his back, touching his toes. Then he picked each leg up by the foot to stretch his quads while the other two ushered Greer out at gunpoint.

"Well, here we are, Greer," the Gardner said. "Let the formalities begin."

"What the hell are you talking about?" Greer's silk robe flapped in the hot wind. The man who'd sat opposite him in the back seat pushed him two steps into the open then walked back toward the Gardner, handing him the gun as he passed. His eyes were trained on the road in the distance. The Gardner took the gun like an old soldier, flicking the safety on and off, centering the weight on his palm for a moment before bracing himself as he aimed it at Greer.

"Are you ready for the ultimatum you're going to refuse?" The Gardner pulled his rumpled shirt back down over his stomach and then checked his bulky plastic watch before looking back at Greer.

"Go on then."

"All you have to do is retire. You and your team."

Greer let out a huff of air. "That's it, huh? Retire?"

"That's it. Millions of people do it every day. Most people work for it. Visit the Grand Canyon or Boca. You know, things like that."

"Don't care to see the Grand Canyon. Hate Boca. Too many old people."

The Gardner laughed a high–pitched, fast laugh. "That's just it! That's. Just. It. You don't know it, but you're already there. You and your team should have been in Boca long ago."

"So that's what this is about? You're some insane fan, furious we aren't winning every fight, every time."

The Gardner shook his head sadly. "No Greer. The only difference between you and me is that you are the old guard, and I am the new guard."

"I wasn't aware that there was a shift change." Greer shielded his face from the desert dust with his hands.

"The old guard rarely are," said the Gardner. "That's what makes them the old guard. And there comes a time when they must pass."

"Don't bullshit me. You kill me, it's nothing but murder. "

The Gardner cocked his head. "Yes… but more than that, it's a *passing*. I am *passing* you. Do you see? You should be happy! Your team was a champion once, in a different era, and you weren't even supposed to get that far! You can take that to your grave." The Gardner nodded, eyes wide despite the dust. "So. I take it you won't dismantle your team."

Greer laughed. It took everything he had, but he laughed.

"And now is when I ask you what you find so funny. What is the single hope you cling to so desperately, that lets you laugh at this hour? Everyone has to have one. It helps to look at death sidelong. Keeps you sane when it's staring you in the face."

"You talk like they'd quit if I told them to."

"I wouldn't be so sure. But regardless, I'm assuming you won't tell them to."

The Gardner centered his aim so that Greer was staring down the barrel.

"No," Greer said. "Nobody pushes us out."

"What did I tell you guys?" Gardner glanced at the driver. "Told you he'd say that. You owe me a Dairy Queen. I told you." He focused on Greer once more. "So that's a no?"

"That's a no."

"A hard no? I want this on record. For the Dairy Queen."

"Fuck you."

The Gardner laughed. "I hope they're half as fun when I come for them, your precious team of washed–up losers."

"You go after them, and I think they'll give you all the fun you can handle."

The Gardner nodded. "Yeah, yeah." He was still nodding when he shot Greer once in the face. The bullet smashed his forehead in and ballooned out of the back of his head. His blood and brain matter misted into the hot desert wind, and Greer fell backward, collapsing at the knees.

The Gardner set his gun on the hood of the car then moved to the trunk to help his driver and gunman with the shovels and the tarp.

Chapter Two

WHO EVER HEARD of a press conference at a funeral?

That's what ran through Ellie's mind. Not that Greer was dead. Not that they'd found an anonymous note taped to their fence that read BANG and gave the coordinates to Greer's shallow grave four miles off of the most desolate strip of shithole American highway she'd ever seen. Not that she'd lost a friend. And definitely not that certain other teams around the world were, if not overtly applauding Greer's fate, then at the very least, not sorry for it.

If she thought about all that, she'd lose her composure in front of the world. She'd learned over the years to focus on the minutiae. The insanity of it all helped keep her sane. And the fact was, after this funeral, she'd have to give a press conference.

The cameras were on her and on Tom Elrey to her left and Cy Bell to her right as all three of them sat in the front row of chairs on the cemetery grass, mere feet from what would become Greer Nichols' grave. They lived in front of the cameras now. They bore them at times like gauntlets and at times like chains, but they always bore them.

Tom turned to Ellie in the middle of a hymn and whispered, "A month ago, nobody knew him."

And it was true. This was a story whipped into frenzy by the Tournament networks. The networks followed the trail from the note to the police report and finally to Greer's body faster than Ellie herself. When Greer was identified as the Blue administrator, the Tournament superfans—men and women who called themselves "wonks"—suddenly had a new martyr: a man taken from them before they ever really knew him, much as Johnnie Northern had been.

Tom's eyes were bleary, as if his tears had washed them to a light blue. His face was tinged with a raspy beard. His hair had basically left him, but in its place, he'd been given a smooth brow and a perfect dome of symmetrical stubble that served him far better than his shock of blonde once had. He puckered his mouth and shook his head in disgust, and Ellie knew his quivering lip would be replayed across the world to the delight of millions of women. That was the way Tom was. It seemed not right to Ellie that at Greer's funeral, Tom would break more hearts than the departed. But that was the way of it.

Cy whispered from her right. "What do you see?" His voice sounded calm, reassuring. Ellie remembered the days when she couldn't even get him to say a word. He was her striker, the strong–arm position, the muscle. In the beginning, he'd buried himself in a gray hoodie and let his gun do the talking. He'd been the one Ellie had to rein in. The one who needed watching. The liability. Then five years ago, he'd married Troya Parker. The press loved to equate the wedding with the downfall of Blue because they hadn't placed well in the Tournament since. But Ellie knew better. The Tournament was getting harder and harder to win. Cy's marital status had nothing to do with it. And besides, without Troya, Cy would be dead. Ellie had no doubt about that. Without Troya, he had no sense of self–preservation.

When Cy and Troya had a child, the press really went to town. "You can't be a Tournament player with a kid," they said. "When you have a kid, you stop being a warrior, and you become a dad. Dads belong at piano recitals, not in Tournament gunfights." But the press didn't see what Ellie saw. They couldn't understand that Troya and now Maddie, their little girl, had drawn Cy out from within himself. Gone were the baggy clothes, the work boots, and the flat, dull gaze that always seemed to portend violence. In its place was a sober–eyed father, a listener, an observer. The fury was still there, but it was in check. Ellie recalled the saying: Beware the fury of a soft–spoken man.

"I see a media circus," Ellie mumbled back, keeping her lips still, knowing that they were being read around the world. "I see a circus at what should be a circle of friends swapping stories about Greer over beer."

Cy nodded in agreement, but that wasn't what he meant. Ellie knew that he was asking if she saw anything out of the ordinary, anyone who might be driving by the aftermath of the crime to see his or her handiwork. Ellie's answer to his unspoken question was no. She saw the same members of the press behind the cordon line and the wonks behind them, many of whom she also recognized. Four people sat inside the cordon: the three of them and Brandt Robinson, Greer's longtime assistant, who looked as though he'd been hit by a bus. Frank Youngsmith and Allen Lockton, two of the Tournament's intrepid couriers and longtime

friends of Team Blue, were caught up on the job in Tokyo, or
they would surely have been there. But even counting them,
the number of close friends Greer had could fit around a dinner table. Ellie knew that Greer was a private man, but that his
funeral could be so sparsely attended and such a spectacle at the
same time seemed doubly sad.

The raspy whispers of the crowd and the chatter of the cameras drowned out the pastor's words. It was enough to make
Ellie's face twitch. She shifted her weight uneasily, her grief turning to anger, and just as she was about to stand and confront the
crowd, she saw a flash of gold from an adjacent hill as Ian Finn's
old Zippo lighter caught the sun. It was one of the ways he let
her know he was there too. Ellie took a breath and allowed the
wave to pass over her head.

She could almost see Ian's steady gaze searching for her eyes,
pulling them up from the ground. *Let the frenzy go on around you*,
he'd say. *They can only get to you if you let them.*

She sat up tall again and found Tom watching her out of
the corner of his eye. "Your beacon on the hill is back," he said.
"Good of him to come."

Tom let it be at that, but Ellie heard the subtext. The three
of them were in the thick of it while Ian waved from the hill.
She knew Tom resented Ian for what his distance did to her. A
decade was a long time for a long–distance relationship. But
Ian was a wanted man. He'd made a powerful enemy in Alex
Auldborne, captain of England's Team Grey. And he'd been given
a bad diagnosis years ago: he was one diode shot from death.
The Tournament diode system was dangerous to begin with. A
diode shot from a standard gun replicated a bullet wound to near

perfection when it struck a Tournament player. It was a weapon that took players to the brink of death but also allowed them to be brought back. For a price. Over time, the diode broke down the players' bodies from the inside, and Ian's body was one hit from shattering. Ellie had decided years ago that she'd keep Ian secret forever if it meant he would be safe.

Safety was a concept Tom had never quite grasped. Ellie patted his knee and eyed him. Eventually, he granted her a sad smile. "I get it. Now's not the time," he whispered.

The three of them watched as the urn containing Greer's ashes was placed in the ground, and they stood to affix the marble seal over the ground. It read:

Greer Nichols

Patriot. Leader. Friend.

While they stood, bathed in flashbulb white, Brandt gestured to them. His pale face was streaked with red, his eyes watery. His thin blond hair was pushed back and clumped, as if he'd sat with his head in his hands for hours. His voice was thick. "This way. They're already there. Waiting."

And they were—forty-five of them, representatives of the major global Tournament networks. They sat in rows of folding chairs inside a makeshift room constructed of four walls of fabric erected in the cemetery parking lot. Ellie had learned over the years that a press conference could be held anywhere. The press primed microphones and camera equipment as Ellie, Tom, and Cy took their places behind a long table. Each had an array of microphones and a glass of water in front of them. Behind them, the Tournament standard fluttered softly in the breeze: a circular T symbol, recognized everywhere, tinted Blue for the USA team.

At first, Ellie thought she might catch one small mercy on this day: Keith Snedeker, the lead anchor for the United States Tournament Network, was not in his usual spot. USTN was the largest and most comprehensive of the global Tournament networks, a twenty–four hour extravaganza of all things Tournament. When the game was on, they were everywhere. When the game was off, they were still everywhere. Over ten years of non–stop air time, USTN still hadn't run out of things to discuss, analyze, and over–analyze. Their slogan was *Stay Ahead of the Teams.*

Ellie stifled a curse when she saw Keith elbowing his way forward. It was too much to hope he'd miss this. Snedeker was a tall, formidable presence in his mid–forties, strong and broad. He wore boring, presidential suits, perfectly tailored to his frame, and had a finely parted, full head of salt–and–pepper hair. He'd made a name for himself by getting interviews others couldn't and by asking questions in those interviews that others wouldn't. He towered over his interviewees, and when he removed his gold, wire–framed spectacles, it usually meant he was going for the jugular. One didn't get to sit front and center in every press conference with right of first question by being reserved, respectful, and timid. Snedeker was a throat–stepper with a velvet voice.

Ellie and all of Team Blue found Snedeker insufferable, but he anchored the most popular television station in the world. There was no getting around him. He pushed his way to his chair, popped his phone from his jacket, set it to record, then rolled his neck. He looked at Ellie and smiled. Ellie wanted to wipe that smile off on the concrete, but instead, she cleared her throat and leaned in to her microphone array.

"I don't have much to say today. Honestly, I don't think I

should be saying anything at all. This is a tragic day in the history of Blue, but more than that, it's a tragic day for us personally. Greer built this team. He saw us through our first championship. He always got us the intel we needed. He was a great administrator and a great man, and he will be sorely missed."

Ellie sat back then sighed and nodded at Snedeker. "Go ahead, Keith."

"Yes, this question is for you, Ellie. Do you have any idea who was behind Greer's murder?"

"We don't know anything about the circumstances surrounding his death yet. I can't comment on any of that."

Other members of the press corps chimed in, but Snedeker's booming voice beat them all out. "Well, we do, actually. USTN received his autopsy report, listing the cause of death as a gunshot wound to the center of the forehead, execution style. Can you think of anyone who might have wanted to execute Greer?"

Ellie suspected as much from the note, but it still hurt to hear the proof out loud, and it hurt even worse to have Keith Snedeker be the one to confirm it. "I can think of about a thousand people, Keith," she said wearily. "It's part of the territory."

"Alex Auldborne?" Snedeker let the name hang in the air for a moment before it was swallowed up by a barrage of questions. Ellie didn't elaborate. She didn't need to. The captain of England's Team Grey had a long and bloody history with Blue and plenty of unfinished business with both Ellie and Ian Finn, the business that had left Alex paralyzed from the waist down. He captained his team from a wheelchair, and he'd done it quite well recently, leading the English to respectable finishes in the last three Tournaments—if not to the finals or the championship.

Better than Ellie had done. If she were to compile a list of killers, his name would be right at the top.

Blue was peppered from all sides, and it was as if the funeral had never occurred.

"Ellie, what of rumors linking you to Ian Finn in Belfast earlier this month? Are you and Finn an item?"

"How about the fact that we're remembering Greer today? Huh? Can we keep on topic here?" Ellie replied.

The press didn't care. In the off season, teams sometimes went months without talking to the press. Any opportunity was like tossing a match onto gasoline. There would be no holding back.

"Tom, are you and Heidi Carraway an item?"

Heidi Carraway was a lingerie model. Someone had snapped a photo of Heidi visiting Tom's house on Blue's compound in Cheyenne, Wyoming a week ago. She'd snagged herself on the fence, and she was barely wearing enough to snag in the first place.

"No, Heidi and I are just friends." Tom scratched at his forearm.

"What about her sister Mira?"

"Her too. Just friends," Tom said.

"Cy, is it true that you and Troya are expecting another child?"

"No comment," Cy said softly. That set the room abuzz. "And that's not a confirmation!" he added over the fray. "It means no comment. That's all!"

"She's not." Snedeker smiled. "Not yet, anyway. We'd know."

Several of the other anchors laughed. Ellie rolled her eyes. *Suck–ups.* Ellie'd always thought it would be nice to have laughter at a funeral but not like this. She felt her anger building again. She caught sight of herself in the playback of a nearby camera. Her color was rising, splotching her pale face. The long scar that ran from her eye down past her mouth to her chin was livid and red. She looked haggard. Her long red hair was tinged with silver and frizzy around her temples. Her nose was crooked at the bridge, and her eyes were dull green, pouched in fine lines and wrinkles. She was road–weary, old before her time. And this stuff was only making her older.

"That's it. No further questions." Ellie stood. Cy and Tom followed. She turned from the table then paused and turned back around. The look she gave the press corps quieted them. It was a hard look. It was the reason that they still called her the Red Lion, even after all these years. Even after all those losses.

"We're gonna find who did this," she said.

She left her words and their implications in the air as the three of them pushed through the curtains, leaving the press tittering behind them like bees in a box.

CHAPTER THREE

IN EVERY FAMILY there seemed to be one pair who drove each other crazy and loved each other fiercely at the same time. Frank and Lock were like that. Except they weren't related. On paper, they were both employed by the Tournament as couriers. Lock was an original courier. He could talk, and often would, if anyone let him, about the glory days of the job when there were only a handful of Tournament couriers serving the world. A Tournament courier wasn't an average deliveryman. They were elite pick–up and drop–off artists. They could be used by any Tournament player to deliver anything, and they were expected to do so within twenty–four hours. Anywhere on earth. Allen Lockton was the best of them all. His nickname was Lock because he got the job done. He was a sure thing.

Frank Youngsmith was not the best courier. He couldn't even honestly be called a good one. But he was dysfunctionally optimistic, and he never quit. In life, those two traits had gotten him quite far, about as far as possible from the dead–end insurance adjuster job he'd once held. He used to sleep in a lumpy twin bed jammed into the corner of an otherwise empty bedroom in one half of a soulless duplex across from a strip mall in Colorado Springs, where, not coincidentally, the suicide rate was one of the highest in the country. He'd followed a lead that threw him down the rabbit hole into the underground world of the Tournament, and he'd had a big hand in exposing it to the public. Rather than packing Frank up and shipping him out, Greer Nichols had hired him. Now, Frank rarely slept at all, but when he did it was well earned, and when he woke up, he was excited. Excited to deliver. Excited to work with Lock. Excited about the Tournament.

Ten years ago, there had been five global couriers servicing the original eight Tournament teams. Now, there were forty couriers for sixty–eight teams, and there were rumors of another expansion on the horizon. Frank found this rapid growth thrilling. He went out of his way to greet new hires, vigorously shaking their hands and telling them his office door, such as it was, was always open to them.

Lock resented every one of them. He thought all of them were hopeless rubes.

Together, Frank's dysfunctional optimism and Lock's curmudgeonly "get–off–my–lawn" attitude evened out into a single, well–adjusted person, which was fitting because they were almost always together. They were known around the world as Frank and Lock, not Frank Youngsmith or Allen Lockton. Frank and Lock. Or if you were to ask Lock: Lock and Frank. They were the men who'd helped Ellie Willmore to the window after the Battle of the Black House. Their faces were nearly as recognizable as hers, even here in Tokyo, where the two of them had been called to carry for Takuro Obata, captain of Japan's Team Red, for one last time.

Obata was retiring, along with Tenri Fuse, his sweeper, and

Amon Jinbo, his striker. After today's farewell ceremony, the three of them would pass their guns to three young men neither Frank nor Lock had heard of. Replacements who were appointed internally. Frank and Lock watched in silence as they lined up on the right side of a dais erected in the fourth ward, an area called Asakusa, which housed the Senso–ji temple. Asakusa was the site of a prior victory for Team Red, and the Senso–ji temple monks had, by association, become the order that blessed the team before competition.

Frank didn't like the look of the new crew. For one, they had no character. Frank thought a lot about Greer Nichols these days and had concluded that Greer had been a guy with style. He'd had character. Now that he was gone, Frank found himself suddenly interested in keeping some panache in the Tournament, but these new guys seemed to have none. They were clinical looking. Military. They wore matching black suits with white ties, and although they bowed frequently and smiled at each dignitary and politician who passed through their receiving line to wish them good luck, Frank saw no smile behind their eyes. These men seemed more like specialists sent in to get a job done than Tournament players. Greer had once told Frank that shooting people was only one part of being a Tournament player. It looked as if these new guys never got that memo.

From his right, Lock nudged him. Lock came up to Frank's shoulder, but he could nudge, cough, clear his throat meaningfully, and in general get his point across without speaking better than anyone Frank knew. He nodded toward where Obata stood with Fuse and Jinbo on the other side of the dais. Now there were three guys with character. Obata's hair was long and black, and he wore a loose Hawaiian shirt over trim khakis. Beside him,

Fuse and Jinbo wore tailored suits with stripes and colors and inlaid silks that flashed in the sun. Frank had to admit, though, that they looked tired, Obata in particular. He was the oldest active player in the Tournament. His face was pocked about the chin with scars, and Frank thought he hitched just a bit to one side, favoring his right leg.

He also stared right at the two of them.

The band played, and the Prime Minister spoke, and a crowd of thousands watched them, but Obata's eyes stayed on Frank and Lock.

"He must really want a pickup," Frank murmured.

When Obata knew he had their eye, he made a small but deliberate sweep of the crowd. His message was clear enough.

"He's warning us," Lock whispered. "Something here isn't safe. Or someone."

Frank re–tucked his shirt, shifting his stomach around. He pushed the few tufts of hair he had left on his head back behind his ears, streamlining himself.

"Should we run?"

Lock looked at him. "Away? You'd better hope not."

"Well, what's he saying then? I'll run if I need to. I'll run right out of Tokyo. Right on out. You watch me."

Lock ignored him. Frank thought it strange that Obata requested both him and Lock. They were known in tandem, but they were perfectly capable of delivering and picking up on their own. Frank perhaps less so, but he occasionally did it nonetheless. Obata knew about Greer's funeral, too, and he was old school.

He wouldn't have taken them away from paying their respects unless it was important.

Or unless it had something to do with Greer.

Now that Frank thought about it, as he watched the three old members of Red in their last minutes on the job, it struck him that they did not seem comfortable at all. They might be standing on their own, apart and in the spotlight, but they looked as if they had a gun on them. Something was not right here.

He shook his head sadly as the old Red were asked, with much bowing and prostration, to present their guns. There was thunderous applause as first Fuse and then Jinbo stepped to the raised platform in the center of the dais and un–holstered their weapons. Their eyes were steely as they plopped their guns on the podium and received a gold medal in return. They watched the new team unwaveringly. Rather than putting the medals on, they grasped them by the ribbons in their fists and let them hang at their sides like dead flowers. Last was Obata. The applause for him was loudest. He walked to the podium, and his lip quivered briefly, an unusual show of emotion from him, which set the crowd into adoring cheers. He seemed not to hear any of them as he flicked off his shoulder holster and then removed his gun from it. He looked at it for a long moment, pursing his lips, then he nodded and set it softly next to his teammates'. He took his medal without looking at it and returned to stand between Jinbo and Fuse, who nodded encouragement at him.

"Call me crazy," Frank said, "but those three don't exactly look like they're thrilled about the swap they just made."

"Someone is forcing their hand," Lock said. "And Obata wants us to know who."

Frank scanned the people around the two teams. They were mostly Japanese, but a fair number of foreigners were interspersed. Same with the rest of the crowd. Men and women of all ages and backgrounds mingled. Red was a fan favorite. The wonks, in particular, loved Red. Obata was a bit of a wonk himself, and they identified with him. Many fans wept openly as the orchestra came to a crescendo and the new Red were given their own guns, presented to them by pretty Japanese women in red kimonos who held them out flat in white—gloved hands to each man.

"It could be anybody," Frank said.

The new Team Red bowed once more to the dignitaries, then to the crowd, and then they holstered their new weapons. They grasped hands and held their combined arms aloft to thundering applause.

"Time for the pick—up," Lock said. "Watch who watches me. That oughta give us some clue."

*

Lock set off toward the stairs leading down from the platform. Lock weaved in and out of the crowd, tracking Obata as he shook many hands with a stale smile on his face. Lock caught his eye, and Obata ticked his head briefly toward where a black sedan awaited the three retired Red members. Lock arrived at the car seconds before Obata did, but just as he was about to speak, Obata held out his hand as if to shake. Bewildered, Lock shook his hand.

"He gave us no choice," Obata said softly, through a hollow smile. "He was going to start killing my best fans, one at a time.

So I did what he said. He's watching now." He pressed something into Lock's hand then stepped into the sedan, along with his teammates. Lock was left stammering as the car rolled slowly away through the streets with a throng of fans following.

When Lock turned back around, he was face to face with a young man in a camo baseball cap and a sleeveless T–shirt. He watched Lock closely then licked his lower lip around a mound of tobacco.

"Hiya, Lock."

Lock let out a breath. "Jesus, Willy. No need to sneak up on me like that."

"Just wondering what you're doing here."

"Obata called Frank and me to one last pick up. You know that."

"That's funny, seein' as this is my territory and everything."

"It was a personal request. Not that I need to explain myself to you. And this isn't *your territory*. You go where you're assigned." Lock tried in vain to make himself look tall. Willy Booker had a good five inches on him, and he wore cowboy boots on top of that.

"Well?" Willy asked.

"Well what?"

"Where's the delivery?"

Lock made a conscious effort not to squeeze his right hand. "He changed his mind."

"That so?"

"Yeah, *that so*." Lock decided to go on the offensive. "And try not to get me or Frank called out to *your territory* for nothing again." Lock spun on his heels and did his best to look disgruntled as he tromped back to where Frank waited. Willy peered after him for a moment then turned to watch the sedan fade into the crowd. He spit a gob of tobacco juice on the ground, to the horror of several nearby Japanese.

Lock reached Frank and quieted him with a look. "Keep walking."

Frank swung around and followed him. "What happened? Where's the package?"

"I got it."

"What? Did you drop it or something?"

"Just keep walking, Frank."

"Was that Willy Booker?" Frank pumped his arms to keep up.

"Yes. Unfortunately." Lock checked behind him.

"What's that hick doing out here? There aren't a lot of cows to tip in Tokyo, and the ones they do have are super, super expensive."

"Apparently he was assigned here, although I don't remember doing it. He's always been a bit paranoid about losing his job."

"He should be." Frank blotted at his forehead with a thin tissue, soaking it through. "He sucks at it."

"The guy fulfills his orders," Lock said. "Somehow." He stuffed his balled fist into his pocket. "Did you see anything? Anyone watching me with Obata?"

"Hard to say. A lot of people had their eyes on the two of

you. There was one guy, though. When the rest of the people on stage followed Obata's car out or turned to the new guys, he watched you. I think he might have spoken into an earpiece."

"Did you recognize him?"

"No. But it was weird." Frank slowed Lock down with a touch now that they were beyond the ceremony crowd and back into the everyday crowd of Tokyo. He huffed, hands on his hips, then picked another tiny tissue from his travel packet to wipe his forehead. "Everyone else up there was in a suit or something fancy. This guy was in cargo shorts and running shoes and glossy polo."

The two of them stopped in front of their subway station. Express service to Narita Airport.

"So you'd recognize him again if you saw him?"

"Oh yeah. He looked like a baseball coach."

"Good." Lock had learned over the years to trust Frank's instincts. They usually led them in the right direction, even if it was via a few roundabouts.

"So where's the package?" Frank asked again. "And where does he want it to go?"

Lock assured himself that they were in a lonely corner of the platform then took his fist from his pocket. "It's right here. And I think he meant it for us to see." He unfurled his fingers. There, in the palm of his hand, were the dried remains of a crushed yellow rose.

CHAPTER FOUR

ALEX AULDBORNE, THE captain of England's Team Grey, had an assistant for almost everything. He had one to help him to and from his bed and one who helped him in and out of the shower and toilet. He had another to dress him and one who followed his wheelchair throughout the day (it was mechanical and of the latest variety) to assure that his overall appearance remained impeccable. These assistants moved silently among Auldborne and his teammates like trained wraiths.

When Ian Finn had tumbled with Auldborne from the second–story window of the Black House, ten years ago, Ian Finn had a lucky landing, and Alex Auldborne did not. Ian Finn had been spirited away and injected with adrenalin to negate the effects of the diodes before what would surely have been his final coma overtook his body. Alex Auldborne had been left broken on the trampled grass of the lawn with his spinal cord severed. He was told immediately upon his revival that he would never walk again. He threw a bedside vase through the bay window of his family's estate in Hyde Park, where he recovered in what was essentially a transplanted hospital, and then immediately regretted it. He passed out from the pain, but the doctors took it as a good sign that his upper body was almost entirely unaffected. His lower body, however, was a total loss.

When his striker, a hulking Jamaican–Englishman named Draden Tate, and his sweeper, a deadly doll of a woman named Christina Stoke, first came to see him, he told them to go—not just from his sight but away from him forever. He was broken. He was worthless to them. The two of them might salvage a team out of all of this mess, but he was a hanger–on now. He wouldn't abide by their charity.

Draden Tate just laughed.

Auldborne insisted he was serious. If the tables were turned, he said, and he was in their shoes, he wouldn't hesitate to abandon himself. In fact, if they wanted to do him a favor, they ought to just shoot him like a lamed horse. That's what he'd do in their place.

Christina Stoke gave him a wry smile. "You've quite the attitude for a lamed horse. Be a shame to shoot you just yet."

Auldborne raked the shadowy stubble on his angled face and pushed and pulled at his hair, flaring it out like a badger. "What don't you understand about go the fuck away and leave me to die in peace and luxury?"

Draden Tate ignored him. He'd flashed the same smile that split his face the day they'd first signed on together: a quiet snarl, like pulling up the lip of a sleepy tiger.

"You want to get the people who did this to you or not, Alex?" he asked, by which he meant Ellie Willmore and Ian Finn.

"They won. It's over."

"'Dis a long game," Tate said.

Alex looked up at them. "You're serious? You aren't disgusted by me?"

"Only one disgusted by you is you," Tate said.

"You'll have to learn to carry yourself, of course," Stoke said.

"Of course," Auldborne allowed, dazed by their loyalty to the last.

"But the way I see it," Stoke said, "you can shoot just as well from a chair as standing. You always found running beneath you anyway."

Auldborne snorted a genuine laugh, a rare thing, coming from him. His laughs were mostly of the "I've got you now" variety.

"Now let's get you dressed," Stoke said.

Once Auldborne felt comfortable enough in his routine, he started to settle in. He dressed in a suit, always, and often in a three-piece suit. He purchased a battery of blankets and throws of the finest fabrics: Scottish wool and Indian cashmere and Peruvian alpaca in beautiful rich colors and patterns. These he tucked around his legs while sitting in his chair, which was an understated contraption of solid steel with a powerful, nearly silent motor that he controlled with a flick of his hand. It took time, but soon enough, he mastered his comings and goings. He was able to match walk speeds and reverse in and out of almost anywhere in a few deft movements. He had the Auldborne estate entirely refitted for wheelchair access.

When he was convinced that his chair was as unobtrusive as he could possibly make it, Auldborne made his first public appearance. He went on television to say that he wanted Ian Finn dead. He also wanted Ellie Willmore dead, but one death threat at a time. He was aware of the theatrics of his position. He knew how to play a crowd.

He then retired to his convalescence. He was persistent. He threw fewer and fewer vases, paperweights, and pieces of glassware as his condition settled. Then he fitted his chair with a holster under the blankets and near his right hand, his deadly right hand, once the best shot in the Tournament. He was determined to make it so again.

Auldborne knew that winning the Tournament was never easy, even back in what now seemed like the prehistoric years when there were only eight teams. But that didn't make his team's subsequent three losses over the next ten years any more bearable. To his face, people said that Grey's showings were admirable. They lasted into the later rounds in each appearance. Behind his back, the tone was different. He knew because it was all over the news all of the time. USTN was particularly blunt, but then again, they were Americans. Keith Snedeker was the first to publicly suggest, via a loaded question in an interview with one of England's top wonks, that perhaps England was handicapping itself, as it were, by sticking by their disabled captain in an era when the game was getting ever faster and more athletic.

The wonk—*and God bless him,* thought Auldborne—was outraged. Auldborne had to hand it to the English fans. They were among the most loyal. It didn't hurt, he knew, that the English loved a bit of scandal, and over the course of the Tournament's coming-out party, Auldborne had provided it in droves. The world loves a villain, after all, the English in particular. Auldborne suspected that was a large part of why he was still around.

But no matter how increasingly ruthless Auldborne's victories were, no matter how creatively he humiliated his opponents to the horrified delight of his fans, if he didn't win a championship soon, they would sack him. He knew his time was short. This evening, as he did every evening, Auldborne sat in front of the television by the balcony on the third floor of the Auldborne estate, a glass of scotch in one hand and the other absently stroking the worn leather of his customized holster as he watched a rundown of the day's Tournament news on BBC Tournament. The volume was low, and outside of the open bay doors, the heavy summer heat of a still London night was settling in soft waves over the city.

Deborah Becker, BBCT's head anchor, was interviewing Sanjay Paik, widely respected as England's head wonk and a frequent contributor to the program. "One does get the sense, though, doesn't one, that we're gearing up for another cycle."

"It's quite a bit more than a sense, actually." Paik straightened his bulky plastic eyeglasses. "Our people have it on good authority that the draw is impending. And it's not just the Grey wonks. Branches from around the world agree."

Auldborne watched placidly. Although this seemed like news to Deborah, it was not to him. Auldborne had his sources as well. He flipped to USTN, which played *Tournament in the Round,* their nightly report, globally as well. Snedeker was behind the desk, his eyeglasses grasped between his fingers, addressing the camera in his customary Keith Opines sendoff:

"Here's the truth, the draw is coming any day, and this is it for Ellie and company. You know it, and I know it. We love our warriors, but if they don't produce, it's more than an ego blow to the wonks. It's a loss of face for the country. It's a loss of wealth. And most of all, it is a loss of political power. The Tournament is no longer soft politics. It's hard politics. It's the way deals get done. If Blue can't get it done, we need an open, honest dialogue about how to respectfully phase them out for three people who can. They've done great things, but this isn't about nostalgia. This is about keeping the United States competitive." Keith replaced his eyeglasses. "I'm Keith Snedeker. Join me tomorrow, same time, same place, and together we will stay ahead of the players. Goodnight."

Auldborne took a burning sip of scotch and smiled briefly. At least Ellie Willmore was getting it on her end too and worse than the English press, if he was honest. And she'd actually won a championship.

He flipped back to BBCT, where Sanjay Paik was speaking. "I do hate to say it, but it is true. If Auldborne can't marshal his way to a win or at least an appearance in the final groupings, I'm afraid nothing will quiet the calls for his resignation. People want winners. That's all there is to it."

Auldborne downed the rest of his scotch and hissed. There was a time when he'd have screamed at the television, maybe even at Sanjay Paik himself. He'd done more than scream, in fact. But that was before. This was the new era. The press was a hydra. Striking at it only made it stronger. And besides, Paik was right.

And Auldborne might have been worried, were it not for the fact that he wore a dried yellow rose pinned to the inside of his jacket. And that rose belonged to a Gardner, a Gardner with significant power. And that Gardner had struck a deal with him that would silence all of his critics forever.

CHAPTER FIVE

EVERY TOURNAMENT CYCLE was started by the bettors. In the old days, there was one bettor representative for each team. When that country had enough collateral to wager, either through hard currency or real estate or the political equivalent, they would signify their readiness to the other bettors by signing in to an online forum where they waited. When all eight countries in the original group signed in, the draw was scheduled, usually once every other year or so. It was a simple, speakeasy system that worked for almost ten years.

Now there were sixty–eight countries. Soon, there would be more. The wagers had grown to encompass every imaginable asset, from money to estates to human organs to political favors and job appointments and war chests of all sorts across all time zones and national boundaries. The wagering had become too complicated to handle on a nation–by–nation basis. Instead, participating nations were split into one of seven blocks who voted on a single representative bettor, an individual called a Purser. These Pursers worked together in a politically neutral zone—currently in Greenland—where they showed up every day at a command center and monitored their representative countries' wagering intentions. When the countries assigned to each Purser offered up a wager, the Purser worked to match it with a rival team. When all of the representative countries were matched and the wagers accounted for, the Purser logged in. When all seven Pursers were ready, it was time to fight.

The Gardner had counted on all seven to have logged in by now, but only five of the seven Pursers had, and this annoyed him a great deal. His plan relied on clockwork efficiency. When the cogs didn't mesh, when the chime was miss–hit, the Gardner grew a degree more furious.

He took several small sips of water as he faced the final two holdouts: the African Purser and the Asian Purser. "Where are we now?" he asked with every last bit of patience he could muster.

The Pursers eyed him warily. They were used to working in seclusion. But one day, a month or so ago, this man had waltzed into their private command center and insisted upon status updates from their constituents. They'd tried to usher him out but quickly found that the security detail was in his employ. There was no one to do the ushering. It was as if the boss had stopped by, except that as far as they knew, up until that day, they'd had no boss. They were supposed to be silent representatives of their blocks. They monitored the wagers and logged in at the proper time. That was all. They were like sophisticated light switches. They'd hardly ever talked to anyone while they worked until the Gardner showed up.

The next day, he came back and asked for more status updates then again a week after that. He asked pointed questions of certain Pursers: *Have the Dutch given you the go–ahead yet? No?*

Okay. Then he'd leave. Two days later, the Netherlands would give their Purser the go–ahead. Same with Vietnam and Croatia and Germany and Austria. He asked after them, disappeared, and then within the week, they were on board. It was clear that this Mr. Gardner badly wanted a Tournament cycle to begin.

Over the years, the seven Pursers had come to know each other, if not in an affable way, then at least in a professional sense, like a senate, if the senate were perfectly accountable to each constituent. They all agreed that this man, this strange man in black socks and white sneakers with his T–shirt tucked into his shorts and his brown hair cut somewhere between a bowl and a mullet, this strange American man—and he was American; they had all settled on that—was somehow the most terrifying person they had ever come across. He ordered about the ten layers of security in their building as if they were schoolchildren. He chastised them when they were late. He clapped off time with his hands like a piano teacher. He looked at them without blinking when he spoke. And they felt compelled to answer.

"What is our percentage now?" he asked the Asian Purser.

"Forty–eight." Her voice wavered.

The Gardner unclipped his phone from his belt and stepped away. He dialed a number and spoke for a minute into his drooping earpiece. Then he covered the receiver and leaned back in to the Purser. "Singapore?"

"Singapore is not yet confirmed."

"Check again," the Gardner said.

"I just checked."

"Check. It. Again."

The Asian Purser reloaded her screen. She let out a breath. "Singapore has checked in. We are at fifty–one percent."

The Gardner clapped his hands rapidly. "Wonderful! That's it then, guys! We did it!" He stepped back. "You did it," he said soberly, clapping them each on the back. The Pursers knew they had done no such thing. But with all seven of them checked in, it was time.

"Let's cue up that draw!" said the Gardner.

*

While the Gardner prepared the deck for shuffling, Team Blue spent a strange night in their Cheyenne compound. It was one of those nights that had a goodbye feel to it even when nobody was actually saying goodbye. It was still and hot. The wind had died down, and the wind was something that they had become used to, like a noise machine. Its absence was eerie.

Cy sat with Troya on an old sofa in front of the television, but he wasn't watching TV. He was watching Troya's abdomen. "Maybe?"

"Maybe. I'm thinking yes, but it's still too early."

Cy laughed and rested both hands softly on her stomach. "I want five, you know."

"Is that so?" Troya cocked her head at him.

"A full basketball team. That was always my goal."

"Uh huh." Troya rolled her eyes.

Cy looked over at Maddie's room, where they had put her into her crib. He could see her through the open door, sleeping peacefully. They had the smallest of the three houses on the

Cheyenne compound. Ellie had to take the biggest, or it would look odd. Tom's was in the back of the property because he was the loudest. All Cy needed was two bedrooms, a living room, and a kitchen.

"If you want five, we're gonna need to get to work."

"I'm all right with that." Cy popped his neck back and forth like a boxer.

Troya laughed. "Five kids." She sighed. "That would put you well past forty, Cy Bell. We all know that ain't happening."

Cy knew Troya meant it in jest, but it quieted them both. Cy let out a sorry laugh and then coughed. He looked back toward Maddie's room. He slumped on the couch, nodding in answer to Troya's unspoken question. "I plan on sticking around, in case you're wondering. I mean, if you got other plans—"

"I know you do, Cy." Troya smiled at him. He knew she'd made her peace with Cy's position. It was up to him now. She'd never be the one he could hang his retirement on. That was on him.

Cy lifted his eyes to the ceiling, suddenly weary. "I think it's coming again. Another cycle."

"It's all over USTN." Troya's smile faded. "Snedeker's an asshole, but he usually gets these things right."

Cy swallowed. "It doesn't feel good this time. Not only 'cause Greer is gone. It just doesn't feel good."

Troya was about to speak, but Cy threw her into silence. "Maybe this one is the one where I call it in."

Troya watched him as he looked at his hands. "Five kids is gonna be a lot of work, after all." She stilled his finger picking with a sure grip. "Cy, you just keep living, all right? You end on your own terms, but you stay alive."

Cy looked up at her, and she pressed his trembling fingers to her lips. Then she pulled him to his feet, and together they went to their bedroom.

*

In her house, front and center of the property, Ellie waited in the hot stillness of her own bedroom and thought about Greer. In particular, she remembered that infamous day when she and Ian limped from Shawnee Mission High School, away from the bloodbath that had finished the first generation of the Team Blue for good. She'd been cut to the bone on her face, Ian on his forearm, and both of them streamed blood as they walked through the front doors and out into the parking lot to face the crowd.

Greer had been there. He was the first person she saw. She remembered his flat, stony gaze, even as she told him about Max's death. He'd blinked for half of a beat then helped hoist Ian by the other arm.

She remembered his calm tone as he told her to get to the waiting helicopter. He would sort the rest out. She hadn't realized how far his deep voice had gone toward calming the relentless pricks of insecurity that she'd never quite managed to wring out of herself. Greer never even allowed them to take purchase, never even considered them, and so they'd held less power over her too.

She'd often asked Greer why she was chosen. Why her? Why not one of a million stronger women, more tactically experienced, more confident? Or for that matter, one of a million men who might have more bravado? A true field general? Instead, the recruiters picked a young Midwestern girl barely out of high school and told her to become a warrior.

In his typical way, Greer had turned the question right back on her. "Why do you care so much?"

"I need to know that I belong here."

"Even if I could tell you, even if I did know, it changes nothing. You are here. Whether or not you belong is up to you."

And for a time, that settled her. He was right, of course. She could waste time second–guessing herself, or she could get to work. She'd gotten to work. But now that Greer was gone, the *why* question was cropping back up again, and Greer wasn't there to head it off anymore.

She heard a small tap at her balcony window, and she turned to find Ian Finn crouched low as he gave her a small wave. She ushered him in. She'd asked him once how he managed to get to her third floor, detached balcony, and he'd pointed out a treacherous series of sloped rooftops and windowsills. He'd assured her he could do it, but nobody else could, and that was enough for her. She didn't want to discourage him. His visits were all too infrequent as it was.

Ellie sat up in bed as Ian came over to her. He grasped her by the hand and sat on top of the covers. For a moment, he just watched her, probing her face, taking in all of her lines and scars. "How are you?" he whispered.

"Not too good."

He wrapped his arms around her and pulled her into a hug that she collapsed into, and she was finally able to cry, something she'd wanted to do ever since she found out about Greer but knew she couldn't do in front of the cameras. Ian had a way of lifting her mantle of pretense. With him, she wasn't the captain of Blue. She was Ellie Willmore.

"They're saying another cycle is in the wings," Ellie said, her face still hidden in his arms. She felt his nod. "I don't know if we…" She dropped her voice to a low whisper, giving voice to her deepest fear. "I don't know if I have another one in me."

Ian burrowed down to her, her tears wet on his face. "You have to. I know that sounds awful, but you don't see what I see out there. Something bad is happening. You know it, too. Greer's murder is just one of its faces."

He gently pried her away and held her by both shoulders, his eyes glinting through the looping curls of his hair. "Someone or something is trying to push you out. And not just you either. It seems like all of the older teams are getting pressured."

"Why?"

"I don't know. I'm trying to figure that out. But all I know is that you can't let yourself get pushed. You, your team, you're a beacon to a lot of people out there. And to me."

He held her as she propped her head on his shoulder, watching the heavy summer moon through the open balcony doors.

"I'm getting tired, Ian. I think we all are."

"I know." He stroked her back lightly with his stiff left hand, once the fastest in the Tournament, now brittle. He tried to close it into a fist and failed. "And there will come a time when you step down, and you'd better believe I'll be the first one there to help you off the stage. But it doesn't feel right out there without you quite yet. Nothing feels right, except for your team. Except for you."

She lifted her lips into the crook of his neck and kissed him softly. The tension in his hand eased. Ian's hand hardly shook anymore since he'd been with Ellie. But as his tremors subsided, it seemed that hers had begun. It was small, hardly noticeable to anyone who didn't once have the same twitch. It was the result of too many diode hits, the first sign that a player's body was falling apart. As he lowered her to the bed, her arms around him, she felt it like a brief fluttering of a bird in the dust. He held her tighter, and she wrapped her legs fully around his hips as he moved slowly into her. When he was inside her and she was wrapped around him, the Tournament was flushed from their minds. A certain sadness mingled with the joy of their stifled cries because after they came together, when the crashing wave settled, they knew that their window of blank peace closed as well. What was left was the Tournament.

*

Tom Elrey waited too, waited for drugs to kick in and calm his twitches and ease his headache and help him not to think about Ellie, or Greer, or anything else really, for another night. He knew injecting the heroin would smack every one of those symptoms over the head with an aluminum baseball bat, but mainlining gave him the nods, and he was on TV and in the papers too frequently to risk nodding. Snorting allowed him his heroin fix and let him maintain a façade of togetherness, and if he was feeling tired, which was all the time these days, he always had the option of peppering in a bit of cocaine. More drugs, fewer shakes, no track marks. Tom wasn't naive enough to think he hid his problem entirely, but he desperately didn't want Ellie to know the full extent of it.

The parade of women who moved in and out of his house, though, was a different matter. Tom didn't care what they thought. Plus, they hardly ever spoke because more often than not, they were face down on the mirror right next to him, sniffing through bills, often naked. In addition to having a drug problem, Tom had what he called a doing–drugs–alone problem. Cy Bell was far too happy with his life to stoop to sniffing from a mirror, which Tom admitted to himself late one night *did* bother him just a little bit. The only other person on campus was Ellie, and if Ellie saw him as he was now—not speaking as he plunged himself into his girl of the month with a dusting of cocaine on his bedside stand—he'd be shattered. It just might be the thing that killed him.

At least the model seemed to be enjoying it. And it wasn't as though Tom was having a *bad* time. It's not like it was a *burden* for him to fuck models and do drugs. For whatever reason, he'd found to his chagrin that the closer he came to killing himself, the more rumors spread about him, and the more furiously he was adored. Part of him loved it. But Tom hated that part of himself. Still, it wasn't all bad getting his back raked to pieces by the manicured nails of beautiful women. What was bad was the aftermath when they saw how quiet he'd become, smoking a cigarette or taking one last bump as if it were a chore. They slipped out or he asked them to leave, and he'd be left alone with the low, throbbing beats of the music.

When he'd wake up alone on the couch the next morning—or

on the floor near the couch with the music still on and the air stale with cigarette smoke and old sex—he'd think about Ellie.

*

Ellie found herself alone that morning too. Ian had left in the middle of the night, kissing her on the cheek, promising he'd be back soon.

*

In fact, the only one who woke up not feeling out of place was Cy Bell, who rose early, head clear, to attend to the soft mewling of his waking child. That was why he was the first to hear his pager buzzing, one of two hundred and four in the hands of Tournament players worldwide, that went off at precisely the same time, signaling the oncoming draw.

Chapter Six

THE COUNTDOWN TO the draw was displayed all over the world—on the player's pagers, of course, but also on television as a constant graphic during Tournament programming. It showed up on watches and on handheld displays. It scrolled around the stock exchanges and blinked on the sides of buildings along with the time and the temperature. One of the most popular recent marketing gimmicks was the Countdown Box: a locked box, usually the size of a music box, with a digital or mechanical display that synced with the countdown to the draw. When the clock struck zeros, the box performed a five-note jig and opened to reveal a present. The presents ran from a few bucks to million-dollar extravagances, but most of them were toys or candies tailored to a favorite team.

Lock didn't go in for any of these new countdown gimmicks or handheld apps. He used the same beat-up old digital watch he'd used for over a decade, and he programmed the timer himself. The Tournament couriers had just over six days to check in sixty-eight teams for the draw, and time was ticking.

Ten of the forty couriers were physically present at the Palo

Alto headquarters in an outbuilding appropriated by the courier network as a North American base of operations down the road from where the BlueHorse Holdings building stood, now named simply Blue HQ. Lock hadn't been back inside Blue HQ since Greer's death. He knew Brandt was busy trying to pick up where Greer had left off. There was no official line of succession for Blue administrators. Brandt had offered to sit as a temporary admin until they figured out what to do. Lock half dreaded the first time he would be called to deliver for Blue and Greer wouldn't be the one to hand him the package. It seemed unnatural.

Ten couriers sat in folding chairs facing a projector screen. Frank was one of them, of course. The remaining couriers were patched in to the meeting online. They showed up as a grid of faces in square boxes, like the Brady Bunch gone into overdrive. Lock couldn't help noticing Willy Booker, bottom left box, staring straight at him and every now and then spitting into something off screen.

"All right, people," Lock said. "Time to earn your paychecks. You've each been assigned two teams, one after the other. You will go to at least one of those teams. The second is, in some instances, double booked. As usual, the first one to sign a secondary team gets a bonus. The teams are supposed to have been authorized by Tournament Medical by the end of today, so you're free to ride. Every team member must thumbprint identify. Are we clear?"

The group replied with nods, some of them already warming up like athletes, rolling their shoulders and stretching their necks.

"I'm patching through the assignments now." Lock typed on his handheld. "Good luck. Get it done."

As the couriers received their assignments, they signed off. A few conferred with each other, swapping strategies and best routes. Some stood and left immediately. Willy Booker lingered on the screen so long that Lock shot him a withering look. Willy laughed, showing stained teeth, and signed off.

"What is with that guy?" Frank sauntered over to Lock.

"Typical alpha male," Lock said. "Insecurities masked by overt aggression toward what he perceives as a beta male."

"You?"

"I guess."

"I don't think you're very beta," Frank said. "You're weird, but I think it's kind of an alpha weird."

Lock pursed his lips and looked up at Frank. "Thank you? I guess?"

"If anything, I'm beta," Frank said. "Or ceta. Whatever the C version is."

"It's Greek. It would be gamma. And I don't think you're classifiable, Frank. You're off the charts." Lock hid a smile as he shut down his equipment.

"Why'd you give me the new Team White?" Frank asked. "I hate those guys. They're alpha for sure. They don't like gammas."

"You don't have to be their friend. Just get them to press the button."

"And where are you off to?" Frank packed his trusty windbreaker away into his travelling bag for Mexico.

Lock zipped his track jacket to the top and ran his pinkie fingernail down the part in his hair. "I'm going to Russia. I want to see what our old friend Mazaryk has to say about our little flower problem."

*

Frank had been right to shed the windbreaker. If he had his way, he'd shed his shirt, too. And his pants. But he doubted that would go over well on Telemundo Torneo, which had no fewer than five broadcast trucks camped outside of the Team White compound by the time he reached it.

The old Team White compound owned by Diego Vega had been a charming place. It was built around his own house, a small bungalow in the Santa Maria developments outside of Mexico City, and even when he bought the surrounding houses as buffers, and even when he put up the rod iron fence, it still kept that humble, family core. Four years ago, Vega and his team retired, and what had replaced them was, in Frank's opinion, an embarrassment, something out of a flashy music video.

Frank should have guessed things were going south when the team chose a mansion outside of Cancun as their home: a massive, columned, ex–cartel boss's house. It was essentially a Mexican Parthenon. And as for the three men who occupied it, it would be fair to say that they weren't far removed from the cartel themselves. If Frank believed the rumors, they weren't removed at all. They certainly had the egos to match the house.

Frank pressed the big gold buzzer on the outer gate and heard a medley through the speakers. The camera above the keypad focused briefly in and out, and Frank gave a half–hearted wave. The gate unlocked with a buzzing click, and two men with rifles stationed inside waved him in. Frank hitched up his pants and started walking. He knew that nobody would come to greet him the way Diego used to. It was one of many differences between the old and the new.

The men called themselves El Tri, co–opting the Mexican national football team's nickname. As far as Frank knew, they didn't have real names, which was another thing that he found off–putting. That was becoming more and more frequent in the new teams. *Nobody's too cool for a name*, Frank thought. *Even Prince has a name.* On the registry, the members of Team White were simply listed by their positions: Captain, Striker, and Sweeper.

The captain—a broad, muscled man with a shaved head, wearing a white sleeveless tee and white jeans—opened the door. His partners were dressed in similar stark white, which offset the myriad of tattoos on each of them, from fingertip to neck and even onto the captain's head. Frank had no idea what their team insignia was. It could be any one of those tattoos. It seemed they had new ones every time they appeared on television.

"Hi," Frank said. "Tournament courier here for your check–in."

They stared at him.

"I'm doing great, thanks. A little warm, maybe," Frank continued, plowing through. "Anyway, we got your medical screening, everything checks out, just need your fingertips."

The sweeper came up first, snatched the handheld from Frank, and pressed down hard.

"Take it easy." Frank chuckled nervously. "My handheld is not your enemy."

The screen beeped, and the sweeper passed it to the striker then glared out at the cameras amassed behind the fence.

"I dig the matching white," Frank said. "The press'll eat that up. Color coordination is important."

No response.

The captain was last. He stared at Frank and held out his index finger silently. Frank awkwardly pushed his handheld up under the fingertip. Frank waited. He smiled wanly. "Could be all that ink gettin' in the way of the sensor. Know what I mean?"

Silence.

"Of course you do." Frank answered himself.

The handheld beeped.

"Well, this has been a fun chat. As always. Charming. But I've got to go. I pronounce you checked in and all that jazz. Goodbye."

Frank turned away and managed to keep himself from trotting back down and out of the compound. It was more than the hard eyes of Team White that had him spooked. The captain had a brand new tattoo on his forefinger, from knuckle to fingernail. Normally, Frank wouldn't have cared, but in light of recent events, he couldn't help noticing.

It was a yellow rose.

*

Lock found Eddie Mazaryk and Team Black remarkably easily, which was one of the many things Lock took as a warning sign.

In the past, Mazaryk had made Lock work to find him. It was a game Mazaryk liked to play, one that both annoyed Lock and got him fired up for the chase. Lock never could refuse a

challenge. But now, it seemed Black was tired of issuing chal-
lenges. They were staying on the top floor of a Moscow hotel,
where they had refused the establishment's services—including
cleaning—and insisted that were not to be disturbed for any
reason.

Lock was announced by a wary desk clerk, who looked terrified even to be calling the top floor. Upon approval, Lock was
allowed to access the penthouse via a private elevator. When he
stepped out on the top floor, the dead silence, sparse lighting,
and pervasive smell of dust reminded him unsettlingly of a horror movie. He walked down a hallway of empty rooms toward
the suites. In the past, Lock had been intimidated by the set-
tings he found Mazaryk in—even a touch afraid—but these
days, there was more of an air of neglect surrounding the team
than anything. Lock knocked on the door of a room labeled The
Roosevelt Suite in English on a brass plaque to the right of the
door. A familiar face appeared as the door opened.

Goran Brander had greeted Lock for over a decade. The
Russian striker was easily the tallest man Lock had ever met in
person, standing over six feet, seven inches. He'd had the strength
to chuck statues, so it was shocking to find him using a cane
these days. The cane was wood shot through with steel, built for
a big man to rest big weight upon.

"Hello, Lock." Brander's voice still resonated, and his shoulders were still nearly as broad as the door he ducked his head
under in greeting, but Lock couldn't help noticing the lines on
his hawkish face and the streaks of gray in his hair. "That time
again?" he asked congenially. His English was nearly flawless.

"That time again, Brander. May I come in?"

"Of course. Of course."

Inside, Eddie Mazaryk, captain of Team Black, watched the Tournament networks on multiple screens. The entire suite glowed electric blue. Mazaryk looked much the same as he had ten years earlier when he suffered his first loss at the hands of Ellie Willmore in the Battle of the Black House. He was small and compact with a smooth, feline face and was dressed in a tightly tailored black suit with matching tie. His hair had changed the most—the long brown strands were gone. In its place was close-cropped gray, just like his father's. His eyes, once as sharp as cut diamonds, were now more akin to diamonds in the rough.

He was focusing on a USTN program featuring Sarah Walcott, the daughter of Doctor Baxter Walcott, one of the lead development scientists for the diode system. Baxter had gone off the grid in recent years, riddled with guilt about the system he'd developed that allowed Tournament players to shoot each other again and again, to survive sustained comas, and to recover to fight again.

The problem was that diode hits wreaked havoc on the players' circulatory systems and were known to cause vascular bruising. In Baxter's eyes, the price to play was too high. Sarah spoke on his behalf and increasingly at her own behest because her father no longer wanted to associate with the Tournament.

Sarah was speaking about what the wonks had come to call the booster shot, a serum that helped speed the recovery from diode wounds but only on the surface. It lessened the ultra-hangover symptoms of a diode coma, but it had the unfortunate side effect of letting players go faster and harder than they should—essentially turning them into kids who never felt that the stove was hot and left their hands sizzling. The booster shot was legal in the Tournament because everything was legal. It had been developed from an immunity present in Ian Finn's blood, and it was key to Ellie's win at the Battle of the Black House. Sarah was at the forefront of a movement aimed at educating the public about the dangers of the booster shot.

"You know, I took that shot three years ago." Mazaryk spoke to Lock without turning to acknowledge him.

"Everybody took the shot," Lock said. "It got so you were doomed without it in Tournament play."

Mazaryk nodded. "And what do you suppose comes after the shot, Allen? Because something will. What is the next thing we will be doomed without?" He stood slowly, taking care not to crack stressed joints or twinge frayed muscles as he turned to face Lock. "And I wonder, will we all take it?"

"If it means winning, I guess I'd have to say yes."

Mazaryk nodded, lost in thought. In the far corner, Ales Radomir, Black's silent sweeper, watched Lock from a puffy chair. His customary round spectacles rested on the armrest at his right. Lock had never realized how small and puffy the sweeper's eyes were without their lenses set like mirrors against the flat wall of his face.

"And what if it means simply surviving?" Mazaryk asked.

"I don't know, Eddie. There's always retirement." As soon as it left his mouth, Lock regretted saying it. This man and his team had been more than a thorn in his side for years—they had often been a knife at his back and at the backs of Blue and many other teams— but it frightened him that, in this moment, he would prefer to see a man like Eddie Mazaryk compete than any of the new teams. Mazaryk was ruthless, or used to be, but at least he had a code, a code Lock knew and trusted. Mazaryk wasn't in it for glory alone. He loved the Tournament. His father had created the Tournament. It was in his blood.

Mazaryk chuckled softly. "Retire? Not yet, Allen. When that day comes, you won't find me holed up in a hotel, hovering over Moscow like an old fly. When I want to disappear, you'll never see me again."

Lock didn't doubt it. He handed Mazaryk the handheld and watched as Mazaryk thumbed it. When it beeped, the captain seemed not to notice, as if his mind were already elsewhere. Only when Brander took the device from his hands did Mazaryk look up again. In the complete silence of the hotel suite, it was almost as if Lock could hear the man thinking.

"Say, Eddie," Lock began, haltingly. "There's been this symbol going around. Sort of like… popping up, and it worries me—"

"The yellow rose," Mazaryk said without hesitation. Ales shifted in his chair, the first indication Lock had that he was even awake.

"It worries me too," Mazaryk said softly, which Lock realized was exactly the opposite of what he'd wanted Mazaryk to say.

"You know, it sounds strange," Lock said, forcing a laugh, "but part of me really hoped it was some crazy thing you were behind."

"No. I have nothing to do with this. Nor do I know the man who does. Although I have seen him."

"You have?"

"Yes." Mazaryk touched his fingertips together. "He stood right there, where you stand now, and he offered me a deal."

"Let me guess: retirement or…"

"Death," Mazaryk finished.

"What? He threatened to kill you? And you *let* him?"

"I would almost certainly have disposed of him right then, but he mentioned my sister. Suzette. You may remember her. You met her in a graveyard once. He mentioned her whereabouts. He knew them intimately. He said he had standing orders with his people to kill her if he didn't walk out of the hotel in five minutes. Then he left a dried yellow rose on the side table. He clapped me on the shoulder and said, 'Think about it.'"

Lock was almost afraid to ask. "And what did you do with it?"

"It's in the trash," Mazaryk said calmly.

"And Suzette?" Lock remembered her—like a ghost, ethereal in her gown and carrying her lantern. She had helped Frank and Lock, in her own way, to solve the mystery of Eddie Mazaryk's family ties to the Tournament.

"She is still with us. For now. My sister can take care of herself." Mazaryk's words held none of their usual confidence. In fact, much of the old Black confidence seemed to have deserted the hotel suite entirely. "But it bothers me. I have no idea who he is. I used to know everybody, Allen."

"Thick guy? Bushy brown hair? Dresses like an American tourist?"

Mazaryk looked up at Lock eagerly. "Yes! Do you know him?"

"Not yet But I'm working on it."

*

Frank Youngsmith was so eager to get his Team White check–in over with that he found himself among the first to log a completion. He scrolled through the list of remaining teams and snatched up Blue when he saw them unspoken for. Then he made his way from Mexico to Wyoming, taking his time.

In a bar in Culiacan International Airport, Frank sipped a margarita from a yard–long novelty glass and called Lock while he waited for his flight. He told Lock about the yellow rose tattoo he'd seen, and Lock shared Eddie's story.

"That spooky sister of his? He threatened her?"

"She's not that spooky, but yes," Lock replied. "Plus, I think you pegged the guy right back in Tokyo. It's the baseball coach."

"Baseball coach. Gardner. Sounds like the guy next door." Frank fished for the straw with his tongue.

"The guy next door who's threatening to kill everyone on the block."

"You think he had something to do with Greer?"

"Yeah. As a matter of fact. I do. There's a pattern here. Think about it. Japan gets the rose, is told to retire or the Gardner'll start killing Red wonks. Mazaryk gets the rose, is told to retire or he'll kill him. And his sister."

Frank pushed the drink away, suddenly soured. "Greer got the same ultimatum."

"Makes sense, right? Only maybe Greer told the Gardner where he could stick his rose."

"Good ol' Greer," Frank said.

"This guy is thorough, Frank. He was a step ahead of Mazaryk, for God's sake. Eddie Mazaryk! And he doesn't take no for an answer."

"Meaning what?"

"Meaning that if he wants Blue gone, he's not gonna stop at Greer."

*

Frank was met at the front gate to the Cheyenne compound by Ellie Wilmore herself. The camera bulbs flashed like heat lightning as she shook Frank's outstretched hand in both of hers and led him inside.

"It's really good to see you, Frank," she said. "And I mean that. Sometimes, I feel like I don't recognize anyone anymore. You ever feel that way?"

"All the time. Then again, I get lost a lot."

Ellie laughed and patted him on the back as she closed the door to her house behind them, and Frank greeted Cy and Tom. Both hugged him like a brother. They hadn't forgotten what Frank and Lock did to help them survive the Black House all those years ago. Ellie often told them how Frank and Lock had carried her to the finish line at the window. Frank always insisted that she crossed the finish line herself. All they did was carry her to the podium.

When Tom grasped Frank by the shoulders, smiling, his eyes were a touch manic—just a bit too clean—and Frank thought he felt a slight tremor in his handshake. And was there the slightest hesitation before Cy pressed his finger to the handheld? A casual observer would never know if he wasn't looking or if he didn't have the type of observational skills Frank had had drilled into in his previous job at Barringer Insurance, but it was there. Cy's hand held the air a moment longer than it should have.

As for Ellie, she looked as determined as ever, but it wasn't the face of determination he once knew—the face of a warrior determined to win. The right side of her face drooped slightly where her puckered scar lent it weight. Her eyes were still a steely green, like moss on an old ship, and he saw some of the old fire still there, but it seemed that hers was more of a determination to survive now, than to win.

"I can't stop thinking about Greer," Frank said. "I know things were changing before he died. But now that he's gone I see it everywhere."

"I know what you mean."

"Tell me you haven't seen any yellow roses." Frank glanced around her den as if a bushel of them might be hidden behind the couch.

"Roses? No roses."

"Good." Frank scratched and then patted down his ring of hair.

"What's the deal about these roses?" Tom asked. "There's been some low-level chatter about them on the wonk sites. Something about a yellow rose being good luck? Or maybe bad luck?"

"You check the wonk sites?"

Tom shrugged. "I'm up late a lot. Can't sleep and all that. Might have something to do with getting shot fifty times over the past ten years."

"It's bad luck. Definitely bad luck." Frank looked around and then behind him. "Look, Lock thinks it might have something to do with Greer's death. And Lock's pretty smart and all, so…"

Cy put his hands on his hips. Ellie didn't seem to know what to say. Tom scratched at his face.

"I don't follow…" Tom said.

"Well, neither do I. All we know is that someone is handing out roses with pretty stiff price tags. Maybe Greer got one but refused it, and maybe it was meant for you too."

Ellie sat down hard on the couch. "This is not what we need right now. We're hours from the draw."

Before he knew what he was doing, Frank spoke up. "Lock and I will take care of it." Ellie looked as though she might question him again, but she seemed to think better of it. The pair of them had already more than proven themselves.

"You'll take this on?"

"Hell yeah, we'll take it on. Greer was our friend too. Plus, I know I'm not supposed to have favorites or anything, being a courier and all, but you're my favorite."

Ellie stared at Frank then smiled again. "All right, I commission you to bring me the story behind the roses."

Frank nodded three times, lingered for another moment then turned around. He stopped at the door. "Good luck, guys. Watch yourselves out there. I think somebody wants you dead." He opened the door and left without another word.

*

Cy, Ellie, and Tom sat on the couch watching USTN as the

countdown came to a close. Troya played with Maddie on the floor, trying to get the tiny girl to giggle or play with one of her hundreds of toys and dolls, focusing on her daughter to distract herself from what was coming. The three members of Blue sat in silence. They had been through this drill before. Speculation was worthless, especially these days.

The camera was centered on a Countdown Box in the middle of Keith Snedeker's round table while Snedeker spoke with his *Tournament in the Round* panelists. It was a newly minted USTN tradition that on every draw day, a blue token of some sort would reveal itself—usually a small statue crafted of sapphires that the network donated to a worthy cause. Then the draw board would fall into place as each team was matched.

As the final minutes ticked away, Cy picked Maddie up and lifted her high up as she giggled and squirmed. Cy hated watching these things. Waiting was the worst. He had all the time to think of what he risked each time another cycle came around. Once he was out there, in the thick of it, the adrenaline and freedom took over and washed away his worries, but until then, Cy was a nervous wreck.

*

Ellie noticed Tom's fingers shaking as he rubbed at his temples. He was the same as Cy in this. She reached out and stilled them with a touch. He watched her as the display struck zeros.

Tom's eyes were still on her as Ellie watched the Countdown Box on the TV screen twitter and whirl and separate into several pieces of molded wood, like a disassembling 3D puzzle. The panelists behind the desk and the entire country, stopped to hear the chime, strangely resonant, like a cricket chirping in the basement in the dead of night. Then the box opened flat to reveal the figurine, and Ellie gasped.

It was a small rose made from hundreds of yellow diamonds glinting like fire in the studio lights. Even Keith Snedeker was speechless for nearly a solid minute of airtime before he stammered, "There must be some kind of mistake here. I think we've been pranked." He let out a forced laugh and gently plucked the rose from the box, although when he had it, he didn't seem to know what to do with it.

"Now the draw," he said.

The teams rolled slowly down the screen. Each cycle, the draw seemed to take twice as long as the last, and Blue was at the very end. They were matched up against Turkey's Team Saffron. As the last team scrolled by, Snedeker wished Blue the best of luck, rather more intensely than normal, given the rose and the lack of traditional blue in the Countdown Box.

The Tournament was open. Their phones rang. Brandt was on the line, saying that if they wanted to make a stand at home, he would clear the way for them. If they wanted to go after the Turks, he was ready to instruct their pilots. It was up to them. But at the moment, all any of them could do was look at one another with Frank's departing words echoing back in their heads.

Chapter Seven

AS SOON AS Black was paired against Iran's Team Clay, they started moving. They were wheels–down at Tehran's International Airport within five hours of when their matchup flashed on the screen. They had plans to stir up the Grand Bazaar, and when the area was roiling like an anthill, take out Clay when they intervened. Mazaryk's thought was that Ahmad Abdullah, the Iranian captain and a devout Muslim, would be at evening prayers. His professed idea was to shoot Abdullah on the steps of the mosque as he sprang to action. Mazaryk's real plan, the one he kept to himself, was to arrive at Abdullah's mosque early, before Brander and Ales started to make noise at the Grand Bazaar, and to shoot Abdullah while he prayed. Iran was a young team. Without Abdullah, they would panic. Brander and Ales would take care of the Iranian striker and sweeper easily.

The problem was, when Black arrived in Iran, Abdullah wasn't at prayers. His striker and sweeper weren't anywhere near the Grand Bazaar teashop they were known to frequent daily. All three of them were waiting for Black at Tehran International Airport, and just as soon as the stairway to Mazaryk's private jet receded and locked, the three members of Clay stepped out from either side of the hangar doors and started shooting.

A newer team would almost certainly have been doomed, bottled into the hanger, shot like fish in a barrel. But Black wasn't new. Black was, in fact, the oldest, and what Mazaryk may have lost in speed, he made up for in temperance. Brander was hit straight away in his bad hip before the three of them could even make it behind a luggage ramp to the right of the plane. He stumbled to one knee, left behind, and Mazaryk knew with a surgeon's eye that his big man was done for. Whatever happened to him and Ales, Brander wouldn't be leaving this hangar. Brander knew it too. With a nod from Mazaryk, he kicked his way back behind the front tire of their jet and situated one massive .50 caliber handgun in each hand, his back to the open hangar doors. Mazaryk's second nod sent Ales to the rear to find a way out of the trap. Mazaryk knew there were doors there. He also knew they would be locked.

"Get them open," he told Ales, his Russian flat and even, like a man reading an instruction manual, and Ales took off. Mazark prepared himself to do what he'd never done before: be the bait.

He checked his diode clip and moved toward the Iranians, pushing a baggage cart in front of him for cover. They kept up a steady barrage, and he heard the whine of the diodes that passed him by and the dull metallic thump of those that struck the airplane and the luggage rack he rolled in front of him for cover, jerking it slightly in his grip each time. He found himself squinting to pinpoint the firing angles, something that would have come effortlessly to him even two years ago. The thought made him pause for just a moment, and a diode rang from the crossbar above his head.

He pushed his emotions further down. Emotions earned players nothing but comas in this game.

Mazaryk brought himself to halfway between the hangar doors ahead and where Brander sat behind the front tire of his jet. He paused and sat still. No member of Black moved, not even Ales in the far back. This made Team Clay cautious. Their constant barrage slowed then paused.

That was when Mazaryk ran. He ran across the hangar at a dead sprint. There was a yell from the doors. He pictured Abdullah outside, seeing the infamous captain of Black, twice the champion, sprinting away from him, and just as Mazaryk suspected, they charged. They ran after Mazaryk, past the front tire of the airplane, and Brander unloaded on them. He had no angle, and his shots were wild, but they went off like fireworks in a phone booth, and all three of the Iranians turned his way in surprise and started shooting.

Brander was riddled with diodes like a snake shot in a sack, but in the time it took the Iranians to focus on his striker, Mazaryk shot their striker in the head. *One for one.* Mazaryk did not celebrate. He ran toward the back of the hanger, and all he could think was that in his prime, he would have had all three.

It was now two on two. Mazaryk took advantage of the time the Iranians spent checking on their fallen partner—something Mazaryk had stopped doing a decade ago with his own team—to meet up with Ales. He found him behind two stacked crates when Ales clicked with his tongue.

"Brander is down," Mazaryk said, breathing harder than he could ever remember breathing before. "They still have the advantage with the exit at their backs."

Ales tapped his own chest, his flat expression never wavering. *I got this.* He gently pressed his captain behind him then took his gun out and aimed carefully at the locked steel door. Mazaryk heard the Iranians running toward them, screaming a war cry, incensed by the loss of their striker. He searched for them in the harsh backlighting of the hangar, but his eyes were blurry, and no amount of rubbing could clear them. He swallowed and put his hand on Ales' shoulder. It was now or never. Then he heard the hissing.

Five canisters of compressed gas were stacked in front of the door. Industrial sized. The type that filled airplane tires. And all of them were leaking.

Mazaryk ducked. Ales fired. There was an almost interminable pause between the clack of the gun hammer striking the diode and the pop, when Mazaryk swore he could hear the Iranians right at his back, but then the back door of the hangar blew out into the midday sun, taking a good sized chunk of the back wall with it. The sound was horrendous, as if the hangar were caving in on them.

Before the debris had settled on the concrete floor, Ales and Mazaryk ran toward the airport, but again they found their path blocked, this time by an army of cameras. As they ran, steadycam rigs followed them on foot while a thumping helicopter camera tracked them through the air. They were bombarded by screaming fans who had broken through onto the tarmac. Mazaryk had been exposed to the voracious fan network by degrees over the years, but still this caught him by surprise, and he found himself covering his eyes against the flashing lights. Ales pressed his hand to Mazaryk's back, urging him on. Abdullah and his sweeper weren't far behind. They were already kicking their way through the open hole and running through the smoke after them.

Mazaryk's only choice was the main terminal. Everywhere else was open space and chain link fences, and he knew Abdullah had scouted the runways beforehand. That was what he would have done. That was what he should have done.

Mazaryk and Ales sprinted toward a single sliding glass door at the base of the terminal under a 747 that was in the process of boarding. People pressed their faces to the portholes on the airplane fuselage, open mouthed as they watched the pair cut around loading cars and signal men, all caught in a state of disarray, some still tossing bags, others running for cover. Ales fired at the door ahead of them, and the diode reaction blew the glass pane into a million tiny pieces seconds before they charged through the empty frame and into the terminal.

They ran up the stairs and into the departures wing with Abdullah and his sweeper close behind. Once inside, Ales looked to Mazaryk. Mazaryk scanned for the exits, tried to memorize the lines of fire in a blink the way he used to, but the camera in his mind seemed to be clicking blanks. He knew he was panicking. He forced himself to take a breath. He pointed Ales to one side of the stairway, and he positioned himself at the other. The Iranians were coming up the stairs. Black would shoot them as soon as they hit the top step. Both men leveled their handguns.

Again, the Iranians surprised them—by taking the moving stairway right through the window to their left. The screams of those waiting to load alerted Mazaryk, and he saw the loading ramp coming at the window like a long–necked bird bent on suicide. The bay window shattered as if a giant's fist had punched a hole right in the center of it, and the crowd cheered in euphoria and screamed in terror at the same time. Ales was closest to the crumpled ramp. He never flinched. He fired everything he had at the sweeper who stood on top of the stairway as if he were ready to part the seas. The glass rained down on Ales. A piece struck him, and he fell to his knees, but he kept firing. Mazaryk saw the Iranian sweeper flinch and sag as a diode struck his shoulder, but he held fast and finished Ales off in a volley of gunfire and raining glass. The Iranian striker stumbled backward, only to be propped up by Abdullah behind him. Both men stepped onto the terminal floor. Two on one.

Mazaryk dimly registered a throng of fans swarming Ales, unconscious on the floor. Four Tournament medics, never far away, had to beat them back to reach him with a gurney. Then Mazaryk was under fire, and his only thought was to get away.

Mazaryk ran along the terminal walkway, trampling everyone who reached out to him, his face a blur in the hundreds of snapshots taken of him from every direction. He ran until his lungs burned, thinking of how he could turn the tide, but he hadn't done his research. He didn't know this airport. He didn't know the exits. His plan had been blown open from the start, and he found himself without a contingency. He ran into the crowd.

Airport security kept the spectators as far away as they could, but when Mazaryk came into view, the fans lost all composure. They turned the far end of the terminal into the worst security line any airport had ever seen, and Mazaryk ran into it like a soldier mired in barbed wire. People pawed at him, grabbing his face and his chest and his arms, screaming and crying, pulling at his hair and groping him and latching onto limbs.

Abdullah found him.

Abdullah had no care for the crowd. In that way, Mazaryk thought he reminded him a little of himself. But that was the last thought he had as Abdullah pummeled him with diodes until he was limp in the crowd's hands.

Abdullah made a show of it, keeping Mazaryk barely conscious as he stepped forward and set himself for the final blow. As Abdullah wiped the sweat from his face, Mazaryk caught a glance of something pinned inside the collar of his tunic. A flash of yellow. It was a rose, set near his jugular. Then, with one final shot, Mazaryk fell back into the pawing crowd, malleable like putty and unconscious.

Black was out.

*

As soon as they had their pairing against Turkey's Team Saffron, Ellie, Tom, and Cy moved to their individual houses to suit up. Brandt said he was monitoring air activity but had no indication that the Turks were coming their way, which meant that they were challenging Blue to move first. No movement in the first hour after the draw historically meant that the teams would fight on neutral turf. The first team to pick up and land elsewhere would dictate the location of the fight. Ellie called their pilots, told them to fire up the jet and set coordinates for Geiger Key, a remote island in the Florida Keys chain. It was sparsely inhabited and open. Ellie wanted a safe, fair fight. She packed a duffel bag full of diodes and a few pairs of underwear and met Cy and Tom at the front gate.

The first sign Ellie had that something had gone terribly wrong was the fact that the media were respecting the line of the compound gates. This was usually the time when they got the lead–in shots, the really romantic and sexy footage that was perfect fodder for gifs and clips and montages. This was when they should have been in a frenzy, pushing against the steel, sometimes jumping the fence entirely. Instead, the media were totally silent. Waiting. As soon as she stepped outside of the compound, she told Tom and Cy to stop.

"They know something we don't know." Ellie saw a woman move among the frozen cameramen, a woman with long black hair, stick straight, wearing a tasseled cap walking behind the front line of cameras. She wore flowing silk and linen that chimed softly with inlaid coins. She watched Ellie out of the corner of her eye with a rakish smile on her dark lips. She was Fethi, the Turkish captain, who called herself the Saffron Queen.

"They're already here" was all Ellie was able to get out before two hulking Turkish men rose like ghouls from the ranks of the media. They'd held the cameramen at gunpoint—silence by force—but now they turned to Team Blue. Ellie heard Fethi scream a firing command, and it was as if the Running of the Bulls had been moved to Cheyenne, Wyoming. Everyone scrambled, Blue and Saffron and hundreds of cameramen and reporters and crew with wonks and spectators behind them. The ground in front of the Blue compound churned.

*

Cy turned back to the keypad at the gate and punched in the lockdown code. Troya and Maddie would know to get to the panic room. They'd practiced this many times. Still, when he looked back at his wing of the property where his wife and child were and then turned forward and saw his enemies at the gate, he was struck with a moment of terrified panic. They were so close. Tom seemed to understand the look on Cy's face and grabbed him, pulling him to a crouch.

"Quickest way to keep them safe is to finish off Saffron," Tom said.

Cy nodded. The gunfire cracked, and diodes whizzed past them, some striking the fence behind them with an electric crackle.

*

All around them, people were falling and scrambling. Broken cameras and discarded sound equipment littered the driveway amid shouts of pain and screams of fear. Standing in the middle of it all, Tom saw Ellie Willmore, open and vulnerable and uncaring, set in a firing stance, one leg back and bracing for the impact of diodes she knew would come. That she wasn't hit yet was a testament to her own accuracy at pinning down the Turks, who were still using the media as human shields.

"Ellie!" Tom yelled, but if she heard, she didn't acknowledge him. "Ellie, we've got to regroup!" He ducked as a diode careened off the iron inches from his head. "Christ. She's on a suicide mission." Tom turned to Cy. "We've got to get her out of here. She's losing it."

"You grab her. I'll cover you. Run toward the town. Away from here. Away from Troya and Maddie," Cy said.

"Start shooting." Tom popped up and ran for Ellie.

*

Ellie wasn't standing in place because she was stunned. She wasn't in any sort of shell shock, squeezing the trigger mindlessly. She was seeing ghosts. Interspersed among the ragtag line of media and encroaching fans, she saw the Turks, but she also saw other faces. She saw Max Haulden leering at her with the same manic grin she remembered from the day in the forest when he'd come close to killing her for what he called "training." Just a blink, and he was gone. Between two screaming reporters and one blubbering cameraman, she saw Johnnie Northern, a man she'd never even met, a man who was dead in the water off the Chula Vista docks before she even knew what the Tournament was. Her vision was the most ubiquitous picture of him, taken from a security still over ten years ago, one in which his blue eyes sought after something just out of frame, and his sharp jaw was set. He turned toward her, and his eyes smiled. Then he blinked out of existence. Ten feet closer, she saw Nikkie Hix, dead before her time just like the rest of her team. She watched Ellie from the ground where a fan had been wounded and his friends had piled over him. She smiled a bright, southern smile, full of sunshine and entirely out of place. She watched the fans scramble for cover, trampling each other and screaming in joy and pain, and Ellie followed her gaze. But when Ellie snapped back, Nikkie was gone. In her place was Fethi, the Saffron captain, her billowing silk and linen skirt glinting in the sunlight. She raised her gun and sighted Ellie, taking time to hone in on her head, and then Tom Elrey was there.

*

Tom almost tackled Ellie in his panic to get her out of the line of fire. For him, there were no ghosts in the crowd, only people who would do him and his team harm. He bowled Ellie over, nearly to the ground, then caught her by the crook of her arm and picked her up and kept running—at first pulling her, then when she came back to her senses, running alongside her. In the distance, they heard Cy firing to cover them in short, staccato bursts of three clustered shots.

"What about Cy?" Ellie screamed.

"He'll be along." Tom pushed Ellie forward.

"No." She shook her head. "He won't." But she kept running toward the Plaza down the road.

*

Ellie was right. Cy Bell was not going to leave the compound as long as his wife and child were there. He didn't care if ten teams came running at him. He would never leave them alone. The thought hit him like a ray of sun out of the gloom as he stood tall in front of the gate, reloading. He would never leave them again. This was his last Tournament. And he knew, as he saw the three members of the Turkish team regroup and creep toward him from three different sides, that this would be his last stand. He slammed his clip home and sighted all three at quick intervals, daring one to aim and shoot at him. They circled slowly like a pack of hyenas, and they seemed to be enjoying it, passing in and out of the crowd, shooting across his line of sight, nearly grazing him, hitting near the windows and doors of the house on purpose. He knew Troya would be watching, clutching Maddie to her. His little girl was probably wailing in fright at the noise.

Cy'd had enough. He spat on the ground.

"I won't get all three of you bastards. I know it. But I also know this. The next person who shoots at my home gets gunned down. That I swear."

The striker, a thick, round man with a long black beard, laughed at the challenge, held up his gun, and waved it in the sun. "Hey American! Watch." He aimed at a second-story window behind him, one that Cy knew Troya could easily be watching behind. Just because they'd run the panic room drill didn't mean she'd go there. God knew Troya had a mind of her own.

Cy didn't wait. He stepped up and sighted the striker, knowing full well he left himself as open as a swinging door.

The striker never got his shot off. Cy peppered him with three diodes before he took three himself. Both men hit the ground at the same time.

*

Tom and Ellie knew whatever standoff had occurred at the compound was over because the helicopters were now following the two of them. When they heard the tornado sirens blaring from the streetlights as they passed—part of the Tournament warning system telling everyone to stay inside—they knew that the fight was now wherever they were.

Their earpieces chimed, and Brandt spoke through: "Cy is down. They're coming your way."

Ellie pressed her hand to her ear. "What the hell happened there, Brandt? We got blindsided!"

"I know," Brandt said. "I'm sorry. I didn't know what to look for. Greer would have known."

She stopped him right there. No sense in wallowing. "Listen, just tell us if they make any unusual moves. You have an air feed, I assume?"

"Yeah. I'll be on it." Brandt clicked off.

"Cy Bell, you loveable son of a bitch." Tom slowed as they reached the start of the outdoor mall. "I always knew he was a softie." He glanced back down the road to the compound and did a mock tip of his hat. "Now that's the kind of family man I want to be."

Ellie, still breathless, managed a smile and elbowed him in the gut. "Right. A family man. That's you, all right."

"Maybe with the right girl." Tom cleared his throat and mouth and spat. He glanced over at Ellie, who looked at him and then back up the road.

"C'mon," she said. "This way."

They ran down the streets of the Plaza, already in a frenzy. Around them, the police ushered the crowd away with bullhorns. Here and there, they were assisted by Tournament security, thick men in boring suits and earpieces who were calling a warning for fans to "stay at their own risk." People heard them but ignored them, like the warning on the back of a cigarette pack.

The crowd knew not to approach the players directly. That was still taboo, and Ellie thanked God for it. But there were a lot of ways to interfere without getting right in a player's face, including not exactly getting out of their way. When Tom pointed back on the horizon at the two approaching figures, Ellie knew that hiding and getting a jump on them would be damn near impossible. Wherever they went, the crowd followed like a school of fish around a shark, just out of the line of fire but close enough to touch.

"We have to make a stand in the street. There's nothing else we can do."

"Fine by me." Tom donned his sleek sunglasses and checked his clip, his boots set across the double yellow in the center of the street. As he unzipped his jacket, Ellie couldn't help hearing the screams and shouts that came his way, and these weren't cries of fear or confusion at the sudden violence. These were the type she'd heard at a rock concerts.

"Good old fashioned firefight," Tom said through his teeth, and his voice was followed by swoons and ecstatic catcalls. He took no notice, but Ellie did. She was surprised by how much they annoyed her.

Ellie and Tom waited. They stood side by side until Fethi and her sweeper appeared down the street, slowing their run and eventually stopping about one hundred meters away.

"Should we wait for them to get closer?" Tom asked, gun up. A shot from that distance was a guaranteed miss.

Ellie knew it, too, but she was tired of getting run around. She was tired of everything these days. She shook her head. "One thing I've learned in this game. Waiting around doesn't get you shit." She turned to Tom. "Stay with me."

"Always."

Ellie ran right for them.

At first, the two Turks stood still, unsure how to react. Ellie and Tom cut the distance between them by almost half before either member of Saffron did a thing. They had expected to go on a chase, and here they were in a game of chicken. When Ellie and Tom started screaming and Ellie started shooting, they snapped into action, splitting up to either side of the street and dashing toward them. Ellie knew they'd be pinned in the middle of the road if they didn't match them.

"Split up!" she screamed at Tom. "You take the right! Take him down!"

Tom nodded and peeled off to the right, bowling over the

scampering shoppers on the sidewalk, aligning himself with the Turkish sweeper. Ellie did the same to the left, jumping up and over an outdoor dining table and hitting the ground with boots running straight at Fethi. The four of them were in a double joust.

*

Tom knew his clip count. Five shots remained. But the space between him and his target was too crowded for even one clean shot, so he used two diodes to blow apart the windows between himself and the Turk sweeper. The crowd was showered in glass and dashed madly into the street, some of them bleeding. But he had his line. The man was twenty feet from him, raising his gun, screaming at the top of his lungs. Tom had three shots. He buried all three into the man's torso as they collided.

*

Across the street, Ellie was held up by the crowd. She heard the explosion of glass and glanced over to see Tom collide with his matchup, and then she was in a collision of her own, with the wonks and the shoppers who were herded in front of Fethi like sheep, screaming and bleating. Some tried to reach out to touch Ellie. Others reached for Fethi. Ellie even heard one man scream for an autograph as she pushed off of him and sprang up onto a concrete planter above the crowd. She found Fethi and leapt at her.

The two women collided on the sidewalk and crashed through a designer display into a high—end women's clothing store. Mannequins and purses flew across the floor as the women landed. They hacked at each other on the polished wooden floor, the stink of sulfur mixing with the smell of brand—new leather. Ellie fought for positioning on Fethi but kept grabbing fists full of silk and air.

Fethi moved under her clothing like an actor changing costumes on the fly. She was slippery, and she was the first to find her grip and set her gun against Ellie's temple. Ellie saved herself by flinching, a mindless reaction that slid Fethi's gun barrel a fraction of an inch as the diode ripped past Ellie's ear and into a glass bay window that exploded inward with the roar of a waterfall.

*

Across the street, the two men were in a tangle on the ground. The three shots still rang in the air. There was a moment of buzzing stillness when nobody approached them, not even the wonks who were running toward the action. Then there was movement, and Tom Elrey pushed himself from the tangle of limbs and stood. He looked down at the felled sweeper, brushed off his front, and then reloaded his clip. Seconds later, he dashed across the street, accompanied by a squealing throng of followers.

Tom broke through the crowd around the store in time to see Ellie shrug off what was sure to be a coma shot, but he knew something was wrong. Ellie was winded. She looked desperate. Tom pushed his way through the door just as Fethi brought the butt of her gun down on Ellie's head, dazing her. Fethi saw Tom aiming at them and flipped herself around to straddle Ellie as a shield. She pressed her gun against Ellie's head.

"Don't move." Fethi spoke with deadly calm.

Tom, still aiming at the heap of the two of them, froze in his tracks.

"Put your gun down."

"Fuck you." Tom said.

"Of the two of us, it's not me you want to fuck. I know this."

Fethi smiled wickedly. Tom's wits left him. He stammered as Fethi laughed, but Ellie struggled, and Fethi's smile turned to a snarl.

"She's not worth it anyway." Fethi shot Ellie in the back of the head.

Tom screamed, a hoarse, guttural sound, and he dropped his aim to run to Ellie as every ounce of his experience and his training left him. Everything went out the window, and Fethi took advantage. She saw his gun hand waver, centered him in her sight, and shot the rest of her clip at him. He fell as he ran toward Ellie and ended up stumbling to the floor. He slid to her feet like a thrown ragdoll, unmoving.

*

In the screaming aftermath, Fethi extracted herself from under Ellie's limp body. Ellie still held her clothing in an unconscious grip, and Fethi plucked her fingers off one by one, exposing the crumpled yellow rose on her lapel. Fethi *tsk*ed. She'd have to get a new one. Then she stood and pulled her long hair back, combing it with her hands. She twisted her skirt straight and walked away from the shattered store with a soft clinking of coins.

Blue was out.

*

Alex Auldborne, captain of Grey, found his matchup precisely where the Gardner had said it would be. The Swiss captain, he was told, had booked several flights to several destinations to disguise his team's approach, when in reality, he was terrified of flying. Nor would he travel by train. Past gunfights on airplanes and trains had made an impression on him, and he refused to be bottled up on any mode of public transportation, although he kept this fear private.

He would wait for his opponents to come to him or to a nearby neutral location.

"So set a neutral location nearby," the Gardner had said, getting excited, "say… Austria. Okay? Let's make it Austria. Someplace close."

"I thought you said he doesn't travel."

"Oh, he travels. He just does it himself. In a car. Actually, three cars. One for each member of the Swiss team."

"How do you know this?" Auldborne had asked. "That's not in my scouting report."

The Gardner waved him off. "Set the fight in Austria. I'll track their cars. You jump out at them like a Jack–in–the–box."

"Just like that?" Auldborne narrowed his eyes.

"Just like that, chief." The Gardner unclipped his cell phone from its holster on his waist, glanced at it, and slid it back in.

"And in return?" Auldborne prompted. He knew information was never free.

"In return, you do nothing."

"I seriously doubt that." Auldborne said.

"I don't lie, Alex. Some things are going to happen. Big things. I want you to lay low. That's all. After you beat the Swiss, I'll give you some pointers for your next match, yada, yada, yada. You'll be amazed how easily you end up on top. You took my rose, after all." The Gardner held out his hands as if he wanted a big hug. Auldborne refrained and instead took a slow breath. He recognized shady deals better than anyone. He also knew they were generally the best way to get results. He nodded.

"We'll be in touch," said the Gardner, already walking out of the receiving room at Auldborne's Hyde Park house. He tucked in his polo shirt as he walked. "Turn the Swiss into Swiss cheese!" He laughed down the hall. Auldborne winced at the joke and at the man in general. He was as uncouth as could be—the quintessential American tourist. He half expected to see a camera swinging around the man's neck.

But he got results.

The neutral ground was supposed to be outside of the city of Innsbruck. The Gardner had said that the Swiss had taken a northern approach, cutting through Germany to deter any prying eyes. Auldborne chose a stretch of the road outside of the mountainous city, just beyond a bend, where he could wait in the shadows of the sloped houses while his team set the trap.

True to his word, their caravan was right where and when the Gardner said they would be.

"See 'em?" the Gardner asked over the phone. "They should be on approach right now."

"My God. There they are." Auldborne's shock was evident, even to his own ears.

The Gardner let out a little whoop then hung up. Auldborne signaled Draden Tate to run the spike strip. Tate crossed the road in a dark blur, and the strip tinkled like jacks bouncing on the concrete. Christina Stoke stood beside Auldborne and gripped his shoulder, her eyes smiling. He patted her hand.

"Be ready now," he said.

Moments later, the lead car hit the strip, blowing all four tires and careening into a sideways slide, rims sparking. The car bounced against the median and raked along the steel for another ten meters while Draden Tate kept pace at a jog on the other side of the road. When the car stopped, Tate stepped up to it, covered his face as he shot the windshield into a million pieces, and shot the Swiss captain twice before the man could even reach for his gun.

The second car hit the spike strip when the first hit the median, but this one slowed and only lost the front tires, dragging the strip out of place with a harsh squealing sound that bounced off the mountains as the sedan spun in a full circle before jerking to a rest in the center of the road. Stoke walked calmly from Auldborne's side, her pug–nosed revolver out. She shot out the passenger's side window, which exploded with an electric pop, but saved her last diodes for the woman inside, the Swiss striker.

The Swiss sweeper in the last car was able to stop in time. His SUV screeched to a halt, and he jumped out with his gun blazing. Auldborne had to give the man credit for his reaction time. He even managed to pin both Stoke and Tate behind their cars. He screamed in rage as he looked for an angle to hit them, so he didn't see Auldborne slide his revolver from the holster under his blanket. He braced himself back in his chair, locked the wheels, then fired once, hitting the Swiss square in the stomach. He went down immediately. Tate rushed over, gun out, to finish him off, but Auldborne held up a hand.

"Wait!" He unlocked his wheels, and with a flick of his wrist, he rolled over to where the man lay, gasping. He looked up at Auldborne with furious recognition.

"How?" he managed to croak.

"It's all in who you know." Auldborne leveled his gun at the man. The final shot echoed down the road and could be heard all of the way into the heart of Innsbruck.

Team Grey was through to the next round.

Chapter Eight

FRANK AND LOCK were at the Palo Alto dispatch office watching the feed of Blue's defeat on television. The camera work was shaky, as always, but with each passing Tournament, more and more of the fights were broadcast using a combination of camera crews on foot, helicopters, and even satellite footage, and they were getting better and better at it.

They watched, white knuckled, as Ellie and Fethi ran at each other and collided in a heap.

"C'mon." Frank willed Ellie to rise. "C'mon, get up. Get up."

Not even Snedeker dared to speak. His whole panel of commentators fell into a rare silence until Fethi was the one to rise. Then Snedeker blew his top.

"Oh my! Oh my! Fethi is up, and Ellie is down! Blue is out! Blue is out!" Snedeker kept repeating. Frank thought he didn't exactly sound disappointed about it. Instead, he seemed almost eager, as if he could taste the firestorm this first round loss would bring upon Blue, the ratings that came with it, the rising price of ad space, and on, and on.

Both Frank and Lock dropped their heads and cursed. Lock put his hands on his hips and muttered under his breath, tapping one running shoe nervously. Frank let out a shuddering breath.

"Dammit," Frank said simply. "What did I tell you? I told you she didn't look good. When I saw her, I thought to myself, *Frank, something is not right here.*"

"You said she probably just needed some sleep," Lock said, his face in his hands.

"Well, yeah, like, five weeks of sleep. She looked run down and tired and…"

"…Afraid?"

"I think Greer's death messed her up."

Lock nodded, but he wasn't convinced that was the whole of it. He looked over at the global courier map the size of a parachute that spanned the far wall. "I'm sure it did, but they got beaten badly."

"They got flat–out jumped."

"How?" Lock stood up and walked to the wall map.

"Well, you saw what I did. They stepped outside and got kicked in the crotch, basically." Frank scratched at his neck and leaned back precariously in his seat.

"Saffron got there pretty quick, is all I'm saying." Lock took a laser pointer from his pocket and flitted the red dot from Turkey to Cheyenne, Wyoming. "I mean, that's not just a jump away."

"Could be they weren't in Turkey when the draw hit. Could be they got lucky?"

Lock spun on his heel and eyed Frank. "That's pretty lucky: to be there within a couple hours."

"Stacked deck lucky." Frank nodded.

"I wonder who checked Team Saffron in." Lock moved over to his computer. Frank took up the master sheets from his desk and started flipping, licking his thumb.

Both men stopped, looking at each other.

"Willy Booker," they said, at the same time.

*

Lock called in a fake delivery order to locate Willy Booker. If anyone pinned a drop–off point on the digital master map, the courier system automatically displayed all of the Tournament couriers within a day's travel of that location. Lock had to drop and cancel seven pins around the globe until he found Booker's signal just outside of Cleveland, Ohio. He was one of three couriers, not including Frank and Lock, who were inside the continental United States at that moment and the closest to the fake pin. But he never picked up the job.

"Get a load of this guy," Frank said. "What the hell's so important he can't pick up a request?"

"Let's play this out." Lock loaded Willy Booker's courier profile and pinged his personal line, the equivalent of an inter–office page. No answer. He pinged again. Nothing. Then he called him. On the fourth ring, Booker picked up.

"What?"

"Are you blind, Willy? Can you not see the pickup? You're the closest courier," Lock said.

"I'm busy."

"Busy? Doing what?"

"Get Sanchez or Fontaine to do it. They're close enough," Willy mumbled.

"You're closer, Willy. You do it."

They heard Willy curse through a muffled receiver.

"I'll get to it tomorrow afternoon." Willy hung up.

Frank and Lock looked at each other, blinking.

"Tomorrow afternoon, eh?" Frank said. "Then I think we'd better see what Willy's up to tonight."

*

There was always one Tournament jet on standby out of San Francisco International Airport for courier use. Gone were the days of gaming the stand–by system or praying for a last minute seat vacancy to get to a pick–up or drop–off. Tournament couriers were given every tool they needed these days. Standby jets, standby cars, standby bikes. Fully packed bags of clothes and cash stored in airport lockers around the world, blocks of reserved rooms ready at the drop of a hat in most major cities. With these resources at their disposal, Frank and Lock were in Cleveland in four hours. They hopped from plane to car and were within a mile of Booker's signal as the streetlights were coming on in the quiet suburban Ohio neighborhood of Bellory, a few miles north of the city.

Bellory was a new development. The houses were large, mostly stucco, and seemed fashioned from two or three different architecture types, rearranged in slightly different ways all down the street. There weren't any trees taller than the houses, and Frank guessed that their trunks were no thicker than his forearm. There were a lot of minivans on the streets, basketball hoops in the driveways, and stray balls in the yards. Dogs barked every few minutes.

"There is no delivery scheduled here," Lock said. "Never has been. But he's in one of these houses right around us."

Frank watched a young kid chuck a lacrosse ball against a bounce–back net across the street. Throw and catch, throw and catch. "Funny, I always pictured Willy living in a conversion van by some river."

Lock snorted. "I wonder if the homeowner's association has issues with his moonshining."

Frank hooted with laughter. "Was that a joke, Lock? Did you just make a joke?"

Lock was about to keep rolling when the front door of the house two down from where they were parked opened, and out walked Willy Booker, clomping heavily in his boots down the long walkway. He had a package under one arm, and he dug out a slug of tobacco chew from his lip with his other hand, flicking it into the street. He plucked a tin from his back pocket and jammed in a fresh dip. Frank unclipped his seatbelt and moved to open the door, but Lock held him.

"Wait. Hold it." He watched the open doorway and a shadow within. "We can find Booker any time. I'm more interested in who he's working for."

Frank eased back, and they both waited until Booker hopped in his truck and chugged off before they stepped out. It was dusk by then, and the cicadas and crickets warmed up as night fell. It was humid and as hot as California at midday. They walked in silence up to the front door, tripping several motion lights along the way. When they reached the wide, covered porch, Lock paused for a moment then stepped up and pressed the doorbell. It rang loudly inside, and Frank found himself suddenly wanting to step back, away from the door and into the open expanse of the yard again where people could see him. But if Lock stood strong, so would he.

Nobody answered. Lock rang again, and still nobody answered. He looked over at Frank and shrugged. Part of Frank wanted to cut and run. They'd done their due diligence. They could confront Booker and find out more, one way or the other. Nothing was keeping them here. But the other part of Frank, the part that was growing bigger each year he'd been with the Tournament, that part remembered how Blue had looked on television at Greer's funeral. That part remembered how the Turks had jumped Blue in their hometown, somehow flying under the radar. That part wasn't leaving without some explanation. If whoever lived here had something to do with it, Frank wanted to know.

Frank tried the doorknob. Locked. He looked down the side of the house. There was a gate there, iron, with a flimsy drop clasp. "Come on."

Lock followed.

They walked over the lawn, skirting the front of the house until they reached the gate. Frank flicked up the latch and pushed it open. Together, they followed a flagstone path until they reached the back yard, a large expanse of manicured green, half as large as it could have been since the back of the property was entirely taken by a sprawling garden in full bloom. The right side of the garden was set in neat rows of vegetables, mostly leafy, in vibrant greens and reds. The left of the garden was for flowers. Or a flower. It appeared to be only roses, an entire array of types and colors, from white to red and even purple, but the majority were yellow.

Frank saw a man with his back to them, sitting on a gardening stool, carefully pruning the yellow roses. He wore a baseball cap with a miner's light attached that illuminated the buds in front of him with an LED glow. Behind them, the gate slowly swung closed with a dull clang that the man must have heard, yet he didn't turn around, even when Frank and Lock stepped to within ten feet of him. Instead, he gently stroked the leaves of one particular yellow rosebud with its petals just starting to open, its base still tinged in green.

"I bet you're thinking, *what the hell is he doing out here gardening at night?* Am I right?" he asked with his back still to them.

After a moment, Lock spoke. "Among other things, yes."

The man spun around on his stool and popped his light toward the sky. His face was wide and soft, his cheeks slightly puffy and red with sun, but his eyes were wide with excitement. His hair stuck out in tufts from a sweat–stained Cleveland Indians baseball hat, some strands plastered on his forehead. He slapped his knees emphatically with his hands.

"I never understood why more people don't look at their flowers at night. I mean, it's half of their lives!" he said, loud enough that Frank glanced at the neighbor's house.

"Yellow roses," Frank said.

"Yellow roses," the Gardner echoed. "I have sixty–eight, possibly sixty–nine nearing full bloom. That's when you have to watch them carefully. It's tough to find ones that will dry correctly. Of those, perhaps ten blooms are worthy just now." He slowly straightened his legs out in front of him, resting his heels on the grass. He sighed contentedly. "You just missed a perfect specimen. Gave it to ol' Willy. The good news is, growing season has really just begun."

"You mean you gave it to Willy to deliver to a team," Lock said.

"Of course!" A yellow rose is for friendship! Everyone knows that, dummy!"

"And what about those teams that don't want to be your friend?" Frank asked.

The Gardner sighed and began removing things from his tattered and dirt–stained gardening vest: a small trowel, a length of gardener's twine, a packet of twist ties.

"Well. If they don't want to be my friend, they have to get out of my sandbox." The Gardner shrugged. "Them's the breaks."

"The Tournament isn't your sandbox," Lock said.

The Gardner pulled a bottle of SPF 75 sunscreen from his other pocket, and then a dull metal .33 caliber revolver. He set these next to the trowel. Frank and Lock eyed it and glanced at each other.

"Now that the sun's down," the Gardner said, "I probably won't be needing this. Though you never know these days! Seems like this summer it's been hot enough to burn you in your sleep!"

He was talking about the sunscreen, Frank knew, but the double meaning was clear.

"Did you kill Greer?" Frank asked, his voice a low growl.

The Gardner leaned back on his stool and let out a laugh. "Whoa, whoa!" He held up his hands in mock alarm. "What are you, wearing a wire?" His eyes glittered, and then he nodded vigorously, and his eyes widened, catching the moon in dull white pools.

At that second, it felt to Frank as though the hot Midwestern night had evaporated around them, and in its place sat a fog of cold. "You son of a bitch."

Frank stumbled toward the Gardner with his hands out, but the Gardner was faster and plucked up the revolver. Lock pulled back hard on Frank, stopping him. The Gardner held the gun between his legs like an empty beer bottle, but Frank had no doubt that he was within one step of getting shot.

"You'd never see another day," the Gardner said softly. "This neighborhood is tough for solicitors. We have this thing called the stand–your–ground law. You heard of it?"

"Frank," Lock whispered. "Not now. Not yet."

"Not ever," the Gardner added, in the exact same whisper. He laughed loudly again.

Frank straightened himself slowly, like a man held outside the bars of the cage but still within the lion's reach.

"Why?" Lock asked. "Greer was a good man."

"I know. I liked him, actually. It's just that there are some people who aren't willing to play my game."

"Like Japan," Frank said, and the Gardner nodded.

"And others, like our friend Greer, who don't want to play my game and then don't leave when I ask them to. So..." the Gardner flopped the revolver around for emphasis. "Technically, they still haven't left my sandbox. Even though the whole world thinks they should. Even though it became very apparent that this is no longer the sandbox for them when they got embarrassed in Cheyenne, Wyoming. You know who I'm talking about? Their captain's name rhymes with smelly."

"Saffron took the rose," Lock said.

"Yes they did. They're a young, promising team. Fethi is what we'd call a five tool player: strength, speed, consistency, calm, and guts. Her gun skills are a little off, but she's learning. It's rare to find a five tool player. She'll be big one day. I'm counting on it. The Turkish recruiters did a fine job."

*

His words popped the bubble of shock that fogged Lock's brain, and a major piece of the puzzle came together. "You're a recruiter. That's why you have the access you do. You're at the very top."

"Guilty as charged." The Gardner placed his tools—all except the gun—into a reusable shopping back at his right. Then he gathered three long–stemmed roses carefully in one hand, clasping his revolver in the other as he stood. At full height, he was tall and big. He had the look of a muscular man gone thick. He looked lovingly at the roses in his hand. Lock and Frank backed up instinctively.

"It's too late for Blue," the Gardner said. "Too late for all of the old teams. I have a poison pill with each of their names on it." His smile was etched against the shadows of his face as he held out the roses to Frank and Greer. "But how 'bout you? Eh? You can still take a rose."

"Fuck you," Frank said. "Fuck you and your stupid flowers. I hope your garden burns to the ground."

The Gardner's hand slowly dropped to his side. "I thought as much," he said, his voice deadly quiet. "Just like Greer. And now it's time for you to get out before it's too late for you too."

Lock tugged at Frank, and together they backed out of the yard as the Gardner stood silently in the moonlight, watching them, his gun glinting dully. When they were out of sight around the house, they both ran for the car.

Chapter Nine

FROM THE MOMENT she was given the recovery adrenal in the Tournament wing of the Cheyenne Regional Medical Center, Ellie was in a hazy dream of half–awareness and sweaty discomfort, like waking up in the middle of having wisdom teeth pulled. All around her were blurs of color and unformed sounds. Once she was stabilized, she was transported back to the comfort of her own home, where she always preferred to recover.

Her first solid moment of awareness found her on her own couch. Her eyes unstuck, and she blinked several times. She was on top of a blanket with two pillows propped under her head. She wore only her cargo pants and a bra. The doctors had cut her shirt off of her at the hospital in order to secure the monitoring equipment to her skin. The television was on, the volume so low it was almost muted. She wiped at her forehead, and her hand came away damp. Her eyes focused, and she saw Tom on a recliner to her left, his eyes on the TV, a beer dangling in his hands and several more empties below it. He turned to her before she said anything, sensing her movement.

"Hi." He swallowed heavily. There were damp daubs of black

under his eyes like sweating peach pits. "You kept kicking the blanket off, so I got rid of it." He turned pointedly back to the television, as if to make sure she knew he wouldn't be staring at her.

The weight of their loss came upon Ellie, and she moaned. "Oh, God."

"I know. It's always so bad, worse than you ever remember it. It's like we have these selective memories that forget how bad that first minute of recovery is so we keep coming back to the fight."

Ellie tried to work moisture into her mouth. The physical pain was muted—the booster shot took care of that—but in its place was a whirlwind of mental anxiety and groggy displacement, as though she'd slept for far too long, through the most important exam of her life.

"Anyway." Tom rose quickly and scratched at his arm, "I just wanted you not to be alone for that first minute. But now it looks like you're all good. Not good, but you know what I mean." He swallowed and pushed a dollop of sweat back from his brow into the golden stubble of his hair.

"Tom, are you okay?"

"No, but just like all of us. None of us are okay, you know?"

Ellie watched him silently, still piecing herself together.

"All right, I'm gonna go lie down now that you're awake and everything. I turned on the air conditioning. On high. It was hot as hell."

And with that, he left out the back door toward his own house. Ellie took another moment to close her eyes. Then she pushed her elbow under her side and ratcheted herself to sitting. She took a deep breath, and it felt like the first she'd taken in a long time. She held out her right hand and saw a slight tremor. Was it worse than normal? She noticed an ice–cold glass of water on the table near her, dripping with condensation. She thanked Tom in his absence as she grabbed it and finished it three big gulps, then she rolled the cold glass across her forehead. Already, she felt worlds better. She held out her hand again. The tremor was gone. She let out a breath.

Ellie fumbled at the phone to her left, pushing the button marked Cy. After a brief series of beeps, Cy picked up from his house. "Ellie, you made it."

"Barely." She heard a crying baby in the background. Nothing sounded worse to her at that moment than having to deal with this aftermath with a baby in the mix, but Cy didn't sound weary. He sounded disappointed but not weary.

"Tom wanted to be there when you woke up. I'd have been there too, but—"

"It's all right, Cy. You guys worry far too much about me. Take care of your own selves. I just wanted to let you know I'm back. Let's all take some time to pull ourselves together."

"All right. Hey, do yourself a favor, and don't turn on the television." Maddie let out a piercing wail. "I gotta go. Call me if you need anything."

"I will." She plopped the phone back in its cradle.

But it was too late not to watch the television. Tom had it on while she slept, and he hadn't turned it off when he left. It was turned to a multi–channel, one of the packages that split the screen into ten or so different squares, each following the current Tournament fights around the world. The first round was well under way. It was depressing for Ellie to see the action going on worldwide while her team was already on the sidelines. There was a spectacular battle between the Canadians and New Zealand at the base of Mitre Peak near the water. Some weather was rolling in, and with the rain, the diodes looked like shots of lightning popping off the trees and rocks in the spume. Another square showed a standoff between Norway and the Philippines in a major city. The skyline looked to Ellie like Manila. They had each pinned the other between buildings across a major thoroughfare. Square by square, the battles went, none of them involving her, or really any of the teams she knew personally.

Another square showed USTN's coverage of a special that they called the *Aftermath of Blue*. Snedeker was interviewing an enthusiastic young man wearing a Wyoming Cowboys hat who was showing off a bright red slash across his torso. Already knowing she'd regret it, Ellie clicked the remote to focus in on USTN and brought up the volume.

"That's right, Keith. I finally got my wings. I just wish it would have come in a better fight, you know? We follow these guys around forever, and this is what they give us?"

Keith took off his signature spectacles and gazed into the camera. "So our viewers know, when the fan contingent speaks of getting their wings, it is a term that refers to taking a diode hit as a spectator—"

"Damn straight! It's a badge of pride! I was just lucky enough to be in the right place at the right time, that's all. I think it was Ellie herself who hit me. I'll get together with the rest of the Cheyenne wonks, and we'll figure it out for sure from the footage—"

"And just to be clear, this network in no way condones this

type of behavior. We've always said that the farther away the spectators stay the better," Snedeker said.

"You stay away all you want. I'll get free beers the rest of my life at the meet–ups, not to mention the chicks at the conventions. When they see this—"

"If we could get back to fight. You said you were disappointed…"

"Of course I was. I mean, just look at the footage. We got manhandled out there. It wasn't even a competition."

USTN cut to footage of all three members in split screen, getting shot and going down in slow motion. Ellie could barely watch. "I mean, you see what I see. It was like a JV squad up against some pros."

"You represent one of the largest wonk communities in the country. What is the sense that you get from your colleagues? What can be done?" Snedeker asked with fatherly concern.

"I don't know, Keith. I just don't know. This is four times in a row now. I think they're done. It's getting embarrassing now."

Keith looked the camera in the eye. "There you have it. We're going to take a short break to cut to some spectacular action in Nairobi between the Kenya's Team Ivory and their opponents from the Ukraine—"

Ellie shut the television off. Cy was right. She never should have looked.

*

In the wake of their defeat at the hands of the Iranians, Eddie

Mazaryk was left with time to do a lot of thinking. And brooding. And second guessing.

After Team Black were revived, they were transported from the Tehran Clinic back to their penthouse floor in Moscow to recover. Mazaryk requested that the hotel staff politely but forcefully remove everyone from every floor at Black's expense, of course. The guests below them went willingly, but as Mazaryk sat in the complete silence of his television room, wearing wide framed sunglasses against the electric blue of the many displays that made him faintly nauseous, it occurred to him that he needn't have bothered. Aside from the headache, he felt physically fine. It was Baxter Walcott's damn shot. It took all of the debilitating pain out of recovery. *If you don't feel the pain of losing, have you really lost?*

The players knew that the diode was killing them. Slowly. None of them cared. The power, the freedom, the adrenaline that the Tournament offered kept them coming back. It was true that they might not have cared even if they could feel the old pain, the old way, but it bothered Mazaryk because the free pass on pain was one more way that the purity of the game was being chipped away.

Still, he didn't miss the vomiting or the feeling that his insides were writhing under his skin. Those moments in the darkness when he swore his brain was tipping over, capsizing in his skull. He'd endured that twice, first at the hands of Ellie Willmore and then again the next cycle. After that, he'd surprised Brander and Ales one day by bringing them Baxter Walcott's booster shot. "It's the only way we can stay competitive," he'd said then. Turned out, the shot wasn't the problem. They'd lost twice more after that, and now they'd lost again.

Part of the problem was that they were getting old, and

everyone else was getting young. Mazaryk wasn't naive. He knew this. He'd even started to sense a tremor in his gun hand. Very slight, like the ticking of a pocket watch, it was not even visible, but he felt it. And Mazaryk knew that there were three people in the wings, waiting to step into his and his teammates' shoes. He still had extensive contacts, especially in Russia, that had told him as much. That these new recruits had remained so far under the radar as to be completely unknown to the press was out of respect for him. Black was the most decorated team in the Tournament. He had built up a great deal of capital with his people.

And yet he was being forced out by the yellow rose. For over a decade, no one had dared threaten Black. Even when he'd lost, Mazaryk's opponents had treated his team with respect. Yet he was being threatened now. His sister was in danger. After the loss to Iran, he'd pleaded with her to go to his safe house in St. Petersburg. Suzette was a proud woman, but she'd also never seen her brother plead before, so she'd gone. Nobody knew its location but him, or so he'd thought. But the next day, a still photo came in the mail, of Suzette in her wide brimmed hat outside of the house. On the back was a note:

Step down. It's not your game anymore.

The picture sat on the side table next to him. He'd been staring at it for hours now. Eventually, he stopped seeing it. Instead, he saw the yellow flower inside of the lapel of the Iranian captain just before he fired, the last thing Mazaryk remembered before the adrenal shot brought him back in a hospital bed in the Tehran Clinic.

Mazaryk knew he was getting old, but he also knew he wasn't the type of old that got demolished by the competition minutes after stepping off the airplane. He had to believe that much. He knew that somehow, some way, the man who called himself the Gardner had helped the Iranians to defeat him the same way he'd helped the Turks to defeat Blue. If Allen Lockton's hunch that the Gardner had killed Greer was correct, and Allen's hunches almost always were, then the man had essentially torpedoed the Americans before they ever set foot on the battlefield. After watching the highlight reels of Blue's defeat played over and over again by the global networks, Mazaryk knew that Fethi had a rose too.

There was a pattern here. The young teams wore the rose buds proudly while the old teams were getting the shears.

Mazaryk ran down the list of the original eight teams. Diego Vega's Team White had retired years before, and Obata's Team Red was out as well. The Irish never recovered from the loss of Kayla MacQuillan, so they'd been out of commission for almost a decade. That left five still active: Alex Auldborne and the English, the French triplets, Tessa Crocifissa and the Italians, and then Blue, and Black.

The Gardner already had his sights on Blue and Black. Mazaryk knew that he wouldn't stop there. He was going to go after all of them, and he wasn't going to stop until they were out of his way. Or dead.

*

Recovery from a diode coma had a lot of immediate side effects, but one that often went overlooked was that a recovering player's sleep cycle was essentially destroyed for weeks on end. After Blue's loss in the last cycle, Ellie wasn't able to sleep more than two or so hours a day for a week. What made it worse was that her body needed badly to sleep. Sleep was the best way to recover.

Tournament Medical gave recovering players prescriptions for sleep aids, which helped some. But more often than not, they made Ellie's sleepless nights hazy and her waking days groggier still.

That first night, Ellie resigned herself to sleeplessness. Ian was supposed to come visit her, even though he'd said she should recover in peace. Ellie had replied that what she really needed to feel better was him, so he eventually relented. But he was late, so Ellie was alone when Cy Bell called her from his house. Ellie snatched the phone quickly to silence its jarring ring.

"Ellie, it's Cy. How you feelin'"?

"Like shit," Ellie rubbed at her face. "Can't sleep."

"Me neither. Never can afterward. Is Tom over there with you?"

"No, he left hours ago." Something about the tight tone of Cy's voice bothered her. "Why?"

"I've been ringing him, but he's not picking up."

"Maybe he has company." Ellie tried to remember the name of Tom's latest beauty. They all blurred together into a taut, curvy caricature in her mind.

"Maybe." Cy didn't sound convinced. "Thought I'd ask. Try to get some sleep."

"All right. You too."

Ellie hung up the phone, stared at it for ten seconds, then got up and threw on some shorts and stepped into her flip–flops. By the time she reached Tom's house a minute later, Cy was already coming down the walk from his end of the compound. They looked at each other in silence, then Ellie turned and rang the bell. She waited another ten seconds as the sinking feeling that had started with the tone of Cy's voice tugged harder and harder on the pit of her stomach. Cy didn't bother knocking. He reached past her, turned the knob, and the door swung open.

"Hey, TJ! You in here?" Cy walked through the foyer with Ellie behind him. She glanced in each of the rooms as she passed. They were furnished with the same basic pieces she and Cy had helped move in ten years ago and looked basically untouched. The soft sound of music on low came from the back kitchen area.

"Tommy?" Ellie called, surprised at how small her voice sounded. She'd crossed her arms over her chest as if she expected something to jump out at her.

"Don't mean to be barging in here, boss, it's just that I can't sleep." Cy turned the corner to the kitchen. "You know how that is—" He froze. "Oh, shit."

Ellie ran around him and saw Tom on the kitchen floor. He was on his side, clutching a rolled-up bill. A streak of powder ran from the kitchen counter down to the floor and dusted around Tom's head. A thin line of blood dribbled from his nose, lurid and red on his pale face.

"Shit!" Cy said again, scrambling on his knees over to Tom. "Tom!" he screamed, shaking him. "Tom! Wake up!"

For Ellie, it was as if time had stopped. She saw Tom on the floor and Cy shaking him, not in real time but as a series of second-by-second pictures that seemed to flash in front of her eyes with terrible slowness, as if someone were holding them up to her face one at a time. Cy shaking Tom, Cy checking Tom's mouth, Cy holding his ear close to Tom's lips.

"I think I feel a heartbeat!" Cy said, and the molasses bubble popped, bringing Ellie back to real time. Cy rolled Tom on his back and started chest compressions. "Wake up, you asshole!" Cy screamed, tears running down his face. "Ellie! He's not waking up! What do I do?"

Ellie stared at Tom's face, slowly paling further and further, starting to tinge blue. Cy pushed and pushed in time with his cries as Ellie bolted to the cabinets above them. She remembered another thing she'd set in each of the houses when they moved in. She prayed to God Tom hadn't done anything with it either.

In the cabinet above the refrigerator, she shoved aside half–full cereal boxes until her hands grasped the plastic box in the far back. She yanked it out and fell to her knees next to Cy and Tom, popping it open. She took out a bright yellow sleeve of inoculations. The adrenal recovery shot. She'd insisted all of them keep some in the house in case something happened on the property. She'd been expecting a gunfight, not this, but it was worth a try.

She popped out one shot, pulled the cover off with her teeth, shoved Cy off Tom, and straddled him herself. She ripped open his shirt and felt the left side of Tom's chest for a break in the ribcage and pressed lightly on it. Never taking her eyes off that spot, she hovered the needle briefly then plunged it through and into his heart. She depressed the back as slowly as she could. She didn't have to wait long.

Tom shot up with a gasp that threw her off of him. He screamed in terror at them, as if they had sprung from his nightmare, then kicked himself backward until his back was against the refrigerator.

"Tom! It's okay!" Cy held his hands out to him. "It's just us! Just us!"

Tom's breath dropped from rabbiting gasps to mere hyperventilation and then slowly down to a series of big gasps. He looked back and forth between the two of them. His eyes settled on Ellie, who cried silently. His gaze dropped to the bill slowly unrolling on the tile like an overturned beetle kicking in the heroin dust around it, and the racking sob that had caught in his throat burst through. "I messed up. I'm sorry."

He was going to say more, but Ellie was on her knees again. She plucked the dangling shot away and then pressed herself to him, hugging him with all the strength she dared and weeping on his shoulder as Cy collapsed to sitting. Ellie found herself kissing Tom, kissing his forehead and his rough cheeks and the top of his head and then his lips, but only briefly.

The three of them heard a sound behind them: the soft creak and snap of the door opening and closing again. A thought flashed through Ellie's mind that Ian had come searching for her here, and she would have to explain herself clutching Tom, but then she wondered what she would be explaining and why, in fact, she felt the need to explain anything at all. But when she turned around, she didn't see Ian. She saw Eddie Mazaryk. With Brander and Ales behind him.

Mazaryk stopped in the hallway leading to the kitchen, taking in the entire scene with one sweep. Ellie felt that he understood everything. She even thought she saw a softening in his eyes, which was why she didn't immediately jump up and reach for a gun. There was no malice at all in him, or any of them, nor any judgment in his voice. "Ellie, I think the six of us need to talk."

CHAPTER TEN

"I THINK HE'S TRYING to kill you." Mazaryk sat across from Ellie in her house. Brander and Ales stood by opposite doors, guarding the entry and exit. Ellie, Cy, and Tom sat side by side on one couch with Tom in the middle. He was sweating and had only recovered a shade of his coloring, but he insisted he be with them for whatever Mazaryk had to say. Every now and then, Ellie noticed he would rest softly against her arm. She was more than happy to prop Tom up. She considered it a gift that he was even alive. Another ten minutes, and he'd have been gone. She wrestled down these thoughts and set aside her confusion as Mazaryk spoke.

"He wants to kill me too." Mazaryk paused as if the words were strange on his lips. "In fact, I think he wants to... remove... all eight of the original teams."

"Is he a crazed fan?" Ellie asked. They'd all seen their fair share of them. It was the reason their Cheyenne houses had turned into the Cheyenne compound. They had five full–time security guards protecting the perimeter, all five of whom had apparently missed

Black. But Ellie could hardly fault them that. If Eddie Mazaryk wanted to get in a place, he usually did it.

"No. I've just learned that he is a recruiter. From Allen Lockton, who was quite adamant that I speak with you about what he and Mr. Youngsmith learned when they met him."

"They met this guy?" Tom croaked hoarsely.

"Yes. He lives outside of Cleveland, Ohio. They tracked a courier on his payroll to his house and confronted him for a time until they felt in danger themselves. They learned that he was, and may still be, a Tournament recruiter, with access to every Tournament resource. Allen also said he admitted to killing Greer." The last Mazaryk spoke with his characteristic, unflinching manner. Ellie sunk back into the couch. Tom's face fell, his eyes unfocused, as if another unseen stone piled upon him. Cy rubbed at his hands, a trace of his simmering glower returning.

"Allen made it seem like the Gardner didn't want to, but felt he had no choice," Mazaryk said.

"What the fuck is that supposed to mean?" Cy asked.

"It means that this man believes himself on a mission. He is driven by a deeper cause than infatuation." Mazaryk unbuttoned his jacket and settled himself.

"And what's that?" Ellie asked.

"I don't know. Allen and Mr. Youngsmith are working on it. In the meantime, I think we have a more pressing problem."

"Right," Ellie replied. "That he wants us dead. But why not just ask us to retire like the Japanese?"

"Would you?" Mazaryk asked, his eyes piercing.

Ellie was the first to break and look down. "I'm not sure," Ellie said. "I think I'd take it to the team. I mean, look at us. Cy has a family to think about. Tom nearly killed himself with the effects of all this. And I..."

I'm not good enough anymore. I'm not sure I ever was. That was what Ellie wanted to say, but now was not the time. Not in front of Black. Instead, she trailed off.

Mazaryk tipped his head. "Hmm. Greer died holding tight to this team. Was his faith misplaced?" There was no malice in it, no accusations. His question was clinical.

"Watch it, Mazaryk." Tom rested one hand on Ellie's knee. "I didn't come back from the dead to hear you shit on my team. Only I get to shit on my team."

Mazaryk's eyes glittered briefly, but he gave a small nod and moved on. "At any rate, I doubt that such an offer, if it was ever made to Greer, was given in good faith. We are past champions, both of us, for better or for worse. Our people cling tightly to that. It is a powerful thing, to have won."

Ellie nodded. "Anyone who wanted to change the course of the Tournament would want us out of the picture entirely."

"That is what I believe," Mazaryk said. "And as for the other remaining teams, I can only assume that they have refused him. Knowing them as I do, I think the Italians are too brash, the French too cocky, Auldborne and the English too proud. I can't think that they would give in to his demands. In many ways, this man reminds me of myself." Mazaryk didn't flinch. "Not prone to asking twice."

"You want to warn them," Ellie said, incredulous. "The

iron–hearted Edward Mazaryk wants to help the same people he's been shooting at for years."

Mazaryk didn't smile. "This man has threatened me and my family." The way in which he spoke made it unclear if the threat was to his blood family or to the Tournament itself, which the world also knew he considered to be his child. "Whatever twisted renaissance he is planning, I want to put an end to it. And I want your help."

*

The reason that Ian Finn was late to see Ellie that night was because he was doing some investigating of his own. He had concluded that the Turks had help, somebody on the inside. It was the only way that they could have surprised Ellie the way they did. He also had another reason to figure out what was behind the yellow roses.

Ian was actively training the next generation of Team Green. The young recruits of Ireland, two women and one man after the fashion of Pyper's squad, had been offered a rose of their own, which was odd, since up until the moment it was delivered to the new recruits' flat in Cork, Ian had been under the impression that only Father Darby, the Green administrator, and Ian himself even knew that the three recruits existed. They'd asked Ian what the rose meant. Ian said that if they took it, it meant that they were no longer driving their own ship.

"So we just throw it out?" the captain, a young woman named Riley with red hair similar to Ellie's, had asked. In response, Ian took it from them and crushed it to pieces.

But he was quite sure that when the Gardner came back

around again to hear their answer, he wouldn't take crushed petals as easily as the recruits had: simply nodding and going about their business. So Ian needed information, and he needed it fast.

Ian, like the rest of the world, was coming to see something in the first round of the Tournament. If you had a yellow rose, you tended to win. If you didn't, you lost. Or, in the case of Greer Nichols, died.

Ian also knew something else. Outside of the people who lived in the Cheyenne compound, only two people knew the whereabouts of Blue at any given time. He was one of them. The other was the reason he would be late to see his girlfriend.

Brandt Robinson had been acting erratically ever since Greer Nichols died. Blue didn't have time to notice it. They were thankful that somebody was there to step in as an interim administrator when the Tournament started up again. They had other things to worry about, pressing things involving them getting shot. But Ian had retired from the diode end of the game, and Ian noticed things.

There was more to Brandt's exhausted demeanor than met the eye. There was a certain twitchiness to the way carried himself, as if he always thought he was being watched. This was partly true because, like all good retired people, Ian was nosy, and Ian was watching. He watched Brandt as he reported to Blue HQ in Palo Alto each day, checking briefly over his shoulder as he stepped in and out of his car. Sometimes Brandt looked underneath the car as well. He looked like a paranoid trying not to look paranoid.

Ian noticed that Brandt had several cell phones—one he used to contact Blue, but he had others. Brandt had a place in San Francisco's Mission Bay, a comfortable–looking apartment on the top floor of a very nice building in a nice area of town. Ian knew it well because he'd spent the past couple of nights at a nearby café, watching, waiting for Brandt to slip up. Right before Ian had been set to leave to see Ellie, Brandt had come out of his building looking twitchier than ever, looked all around him, then took off in his car. Ian hesitated only for a moment then hopped on his motorcycle to follow.

At first, Ian assumed Brandt might be returning to work, at which point, he'd leave off and hop on a flight to Wyoming. When Brandt drove off into the fringes of the redwoods, Ian phoned his pilots and told them to stand by. Ian followed Brandt's car into a remote subdivision where the houses were large and spread apart upon a rolling hill at the foot of the forest. Ian wanted to follow him, but Brandt drove hesitantly, as if lost, and the roads were too untraveled for Ian's motorcycle to stay unnoticed for long in Brandt's rear view mirror. Instead, Ian pulled over on a shoulder that gave him a good view of the hill Brandt was climbing, and he followed Brandt's headlights. He marked the spot where Brandt turned in, waited for a minute after he saw the headlights wink out and no longer heard his engine, and then crept his way up after him.

Brandt's car was parked sideways across the driveway of a beautiful ranch–style house. The far side opened up to rolling, forested hills with a sparkling view of the city beyond. The driveway backed up on the other side to the forest. The house was dark save for the bobbing of a flashlight inside. In Brandt's haste, he'd left the front door ajar. Ian walked right inside.

He found Brandt in the back, rummaging around in a file

cabinet set against one wall of a large office with big bay windows looking out toward the city.

"Unless you don't pay your power bill, I'd say you're not supposed to be here, Brandt," Ian said. Brandt screamed and fell backward onto the floor. He wore a business suit and a head-lamp, which shook wildly as he swung it toward Finn. He also carried a revolver, holding it shakily in both hands. Its barrel was angled toward the ground, as if the gun was a shade too heavy for him. Ian had been around a lot of guns in his life. He knew when a man was prepared to shoot and when he wasn't. Brandt did not strike him as a man prepared to shoot, and even if he did, with the way he held that gun, he had a better chance of hitting the ground than anything else.

"Breaking and entering? And you're armed? I'm not from here, but I do believe that will get you locked away in this country."

"Ian Finn?" Brandt squeaked, his mouth chattering. "What are you doing here?"

"You weren't expecting me, I know. In fact, I don't think you were expecting anybody. This is Greer Nichols' house, isn't it? Or it *was* at least."

Brandt scrambled to standing, his gun shaking in front of him. He tried to flick his headlamp to center with a quick shake of his head but only managed to succeed in dropping it around his neck.

"Yes, uh, this is his house, and I was just... I needed some things of his to help with my interim administrator's position and—"

"How long have you been a turncoat, Brandt?" Ian cut him off. Brandt's eyes widened as Ian stepped forward.

"Get back!" Brandt yelled, his voice high. "Get back!"

"Or what?" Ian stepped forward again, "You'll shoot me? You and I both know you don't have that in you."

Brandt tried to back away, but Ian swept up in a quick motion, gripped the gun by the side, and held it fast. Brandt tried weakly to pull it back to him, but Ian held on and plucked his hands away. Brandt didn't even have a finger firmly on the trigger.

His weapon taken, Brandt collapsed to the floor and sobbed. "I never thought Greer would end up dead," he wailed. "I never thought anything. I never think. That's my fucking problem. I'm not supposed to be here. None of this was supposed to happen!"

Ian knelt down next to him and very slowly grabbed the nape of his neck and pulled Brandt's face up to his own. "What did you do?" he growled.

"He contacted me. The Gardner. Said he was a recruiter. Provided all the right info and said he needed to talk to Greer about getting Blue competitive again. He said it was important. I'd never heard from a recruiter before. They're like the ghosts of the Tournament. So I told him where he could find Greer. Here." Brandt broke down in sobs again. "I led him right to Greer. Right here. And then he killed him."

Ian let go of Brandt and stood. He let out a big breath and sat on Greer's curved desk. "And then?"

"And then... then he said he'd tell everyone what I did, that I betrayed Greer, unless I..."

"Unless you helped him," Ian finished, rubbing at his face with his scarred forearm.

Brandt nodded, weeping silently now, his mouth open. A dribble of spit fell to the polished wooden floor. After a moment, he took a wracking breath. Now that Ian had tipped the bucket of tears, Brandt couldn't stop confessing. It was as if he had to keep going.

"So when I saw that Fethi and her team were coming to Cheyenne to fight, I… was quiet about it. That was what he told me to do. *Just do nothing.* Such a stupid thing. Nothing. Just shoot me. Just fucking shoot me. I've ruined everything."

Ian looked at the gun in his hand and then shook his head. "You really think this Gardner fellow, who is playing teams all across the world like a fiddle, didn't know where Greer Nichols lived?"

Brandt looked up at him, his headlamp twitching with his racing heart.

"You think he really needed you to give him the address to this place? No, Brandt. He'd probably been casing this house for months before you ever heard from him."

Brandt's face screwed up in confusion.

"He played you. He wanted you like this, blubbering on the ground. Wallowing in guilt. So he'd have an inside man by the balls."

Brandt blinked in slow recognition.

"His end game is to use you to sabotage Blue. And he did it," Ian said in disgust. He walked over to the box at Brandt's feet. It was half full of folders and documents. "Now what did he want you to get from here?"

Brandt was still dumbstruck on the floor, mouth open.

Ian snapped his fingers. "Hello? Brandt. Stay with me now. What did he want you to get from Greer's house?"

"Nothing. He wanted me to destroy every piece of paper in the office, starting with what was in this cabinet."

Ian turned to the shelf and stared at it. There were hundreds of files, floor to ceiling, and many more already strewn about the office. Ian walked over to the light switch and flicked it on.

Brandt blinked, covering his eyes. "What are you doing?"

"*We*, Brandt. What *we* are doing is figuring out what this asshole doesn't want anyone to see."

*

Ellie sent Mazaryk away. It wasn't that she didn't believe him. She did. At least, she believed that this Gardner was probably trying to make a power play in the Tournament to control certain teams and garner influence. It was, she told Mazaryk flatly and without remorse, awfully similar to something another man had tried to do just about ten years ago.

Mazaryk had blinked at this and even looked down for a moment. He nodded. "It is part of the reason I am here. I sense some of what I was in this man—the worst part of what I was. The fanatic. The extremist. The very kind of person my father created this competition to silence."

"We've already lost in this cycle. We've lost four times since I beat you at the Black House. I was the one to step up then, but there is only so much I can ask of my team. And of myself."

"You're stepping down," Mazaryk said. By the far window, Brander shifted against the wall next to Ales.

"Look at us, Eddie. You've always been a good judge of character. What do you see?"

Ellie knew what she wanted Mazaryk to say. In Cy Bell, that he saw a family man, terrified to lose what he'd gained. In Tom Elrey, that he saw a wounded addict, a man dulling the physical pain of loss, yes, but also trying to silence something much deeper. And that in Ellie Willmore, he saw a one–time lioness, now barely running with the pride. That was what she wanted him to say.

Instead he said, "I see a team that thinks they're quitting, when in reality they are being forced out."

That hit Ellie hard. Tom even nodded. Cy wouldn't look up from the floor.

"Leave us, Eddie," Ellie said. Anything more to be discussed would be done with her own team.

Mazaryk rose. Brander and Ales followed him out, but before he closed the door behind him, he spoke again. "Ellie, you think you're the only one plagued by time? By loss? History will repeat itself forever, unless someone steps in and stops it. You of all people should know that. I can try, but…" Mazaryk seemed to struggle with his words. "But I don't think I can do it alone," he said finally, and the effort with which he spoke those words was not lost on Ellie. Then he left the three of them to their thoughts and another sleepless night.

His words still echoed in Ellie's head well into the early hours. The team stayed together in Ellie's living room and watched the last matches of the first round unfold on TV. They slept on the couch and chairs that night. Troya brought Maddie over in the early morning, and Tom perked up for the first time in hours, lounging on the floor to play with her.

Ellie's phone rang.

Ian Finn was on the other end. "I'm late. I know. But I have a good reason."

Ellie, who had forgotten all about their scheduled rendezvous in the recent mayhem, felt herself smiling even at the sound of his voice, quiet and measured and calming.

"It wasn't a good night for me either. To say the least." She looked over at Tom, who glanced at her, wondering precisely how much she would tell Ian about the night they'd just endured. She paused for a minute then decided to skip the early events. They weren't hers to tell. "Eddie Mazaryk paid me a little visit a few hours ago," she said, and went on to tell Ian about his theory about the Gardner, which, she had to admit, seemed more and more plausible with the retelling.

After she finished, Ian was quiet for a moment. "A couple of things. First, he's right."

Ellie pulled her legs up under her, shifting the phone to her other ear. "Well, I'm inclined to believe him too, but... I'm not sure what to do with it. I mean, it's out of my hands. We lost in the first round."

"That brings me to the second thing. You may or may not want to fire Brandt."

Ellie almost dropped the phone. "What are you talking about?"

"The Gardner blackmailed Brandt. Technically, he's still blackmailing Brandt. He made him feel guilty about Greer's murder so that he'd throw you under the bus in the first round. He knew Fethi and the Turks were coming, but he was quiet about it. So you should probably fire him. On the other hand, he's pretty torn up about it, so... up to you."

Ellie was speechless as everyone in the room turned to her, their faces questioning. "How do you know this?"

"He's right here, listen..." Ian held the phone out, and Ellie heard blubbering in the background before Ian's voice came back. "I tailed him to Greer's house outside of San Francisco. I caught him going through Greer's files. The Gardner wanted him to destroy everything. I was able to help him change his mind."

Ellie's eyes unfocused with each word Ian spoke. She felt cold fury brewing inside of her. She found herself controlling her breathing. They were played. Mazaryk had suggested as much, but Ellie had pictured the usual interference every team ran into in this game—without—rules. But hearing the proof of it crying in the background on Ian's end of the line was different. The Gardner had gotten *inside* her team.

When she came back to herself it was because Maddie had rolled a ball across the wooden floor toward her. All of them were looking at her, even Maddie, waiting patiently. They were her family, more so in the past decade than her flesh and blood family was. These people put themselves on the line for her, and the Gardner was toying with their lives.

"Ian, I'm gonna have to call you back," she said, her voice steely. "From the road."

"Goin' somewhere?"

"Eddie and I are gonna have a chat with this guy." After hanging up, Ellie reached down and picked up Maddie's ball and wiped it on her jeans before rolling it back to her.

"I'm coming with you." Tom shrugged himself out of the couch. "And shut up about whatever you're gonna say about the drugs. You want to keep an eye on me, right? That's part of the reason we're all here in this room. Well, this is your chance. I'm coming with you."

Ellie didn't try to fight him. She looked at Cy instead. "Cy, you're staying here."

Cy picked up the ball rolling past Maddie's slow swipe and plopped it in his lap, picking up his daughter and swinging her giggling into the air above him. He brought her slowly down and touched his forehead to hers. Then he walked her over to Troya.

"I'm retiring," Cy said, nodding, and watching Troya, who seemed to already know what he was going to say. "That was my last Tournament."

Ellie knew it was coming, but it still hurt. She nodded and started to turn away.

Cy spoke again. "But I want that to be my decision, not this fool's. As long as he's pulling strings, the job's not done yet. And I'll be damned if I let you two go off and finish it without me."

Ellie held back. "Troya, talk to him. He's gotta stay here. I don't know how much this Gardner guy is gonna bring at us, but I don't think it's gonna be pretty."

Troya smiled at Ellie. It had taken nearly five years to turn that smile from a false, brittle facade into something warm and genuine. But it had happened when Troya realized that Ellie loved Cy in her own way, almost as much as Troya did herself. "I'm married to the man, honey," Troya said. "I don't own him."

Ellie took a deep breath. "All right then, let's suit up."

CHAPTER ELEVEN

IT WAS THE poison pill comment that got Frank thinking. The Gardner had said, "I have a poison pill with each of their names on it." Something about it nagged Frank. On its face, it was just another threat. The Gardner was gloating that he had already set the pieces in motion.

"But that's just it," Frank said, when Lock told him as much on their ride home. "That's a lot of pieces. He's practically got a Chinese checkerboard's worth of pieces to deal with here. All those teams? That's a lot of marbles he's gotta wipe off the table."

"What, you don't think he can do it? I think he's shown how effective he can be, Frank. He's already shoved aside three of the remaining original teams."

"But there are three others still in." Frank turned all of the air vents in the car toward his face as Lock hit the highway. "I've heard nothing about any of them retiring. What's he gonna do? Kill them all?"

Lock blanched. "That's pretty morbid."

"I was thinking *obvious*, but yeah, morbid too. If twelve

players, including Blue, disappear like Greer did in a matter of weeks, don't you think that's a little *obvious?*"

"He's too smart for that," Lock said. "If he sparks an investigation that ends up with bunch of bodies, the yellow rose will certainly fall out of favor. The Tournament teams are ruthless, but they don't go in for murder. So he's going to have to disguise his methods."

"With a poison pill. I mean, I know the guy is into metaphors and all that with his playin'–in–the–sandbox crap, but I think he may have been literal there." Frank flapped his shirt to air out his damp chest. It was a hot night in Cleveland. The bright spotlights of the airport appeared in the near distance. Their airplane was gassed and ready.

"And," Frank said, holding up a finger, "if I say *poison pill,* who is the first guy you think of? Go ahead. Spit it out."

Lock furrowed his brow.

"No, no. No thinking. First name that comes to mind. Hit me."

"Baxter Walcott."

"Doctor Baxter Freakin' Walcott." Frank smiled. "Mr. Poison Pill himself. And I'm thinking we ask the good doctor for an opinion."

Walcott lived in San Francisco these days. When the pair took off from Cleveland, they'd take the jet back to California, but they wouldn't be going home just yet.

*

Frank and Lock would have simply called Baxter Walcott to ask his opinion of the Gardner's words if that were possible. But it wasn't. Not anymore. Doctor Walcott had sworn off mobile communication years ago, tossing his doctor's pager out the window of a moving car one day, along with his cell phone. He made a public statement through his daughter, Sarah, who had become the mouthpiece of the Walcott family, saying that if the media, or anyone else for that matter, wanted to find him, they would have to meet him face to face. He was completely off the grid.

He and his wife Sheila, who had the particular misfortune of being happily married to a man consistently hounded by the world's biggest media machine, moved into a one–bedroom studio near Haight and Ashbury in San Francisco, where he'd been staging an anti–Tournament protest ever since.

His denunciation of the Tournament earned him the scorn of wonks worldwide, as well as vilification at the hands of Snedeker and his ilk. It also drew thousands of like–minded followers and thousands more each year. Soon enough, Doctor Baxter Walcott, one of the lead members of the original diode development team and sole developer of the booster shot, became the single loudest and most organized voice against what he and his movement called the "Tournament Insanity" that he claimed had "a permanent stranglehold on the world."

Baxter Walcott's protest movement dubbed themselves the Haighters. They occupied the east end of Golden Gate Park twenty–four hours a day. Most days, Walcott was there himself for at least a short period of time. They kept a perpetual candlelight vigil for every person who had died as a result of the Tournament, starting with Johnnie Northern and Nikkie Hix and moving on through the years, from players to civilians caught in the crossfire. As significant as these eternal flames, however, were the hundreds of unlit candles stacked next to those alight. Walcott's entire mantra centered upon the poison that ran through the veins of each Tournament player, the poison he had developed, which he said was nothing but a ticking time bomb.

"Their candle might not be lit now," he said through his megaphone, "but it soon will be."

The crowd answered with, "The match is at the wick! The match is at the wick! The match is at the wick!"

And that was how Frank and Lock found him: a man almost seventy years old, his sparse gray hair buzzed in a military style, his frame thin and slightly stooped, but dressed in his customary dark blue suit and with his eyes on fire. He stood on a podium and held his eyeglasses in one hand while he pumped the megaphone with the other.

Frank marveled at how the years of relentless protesting seemed only to have strengthened the old man. He was enjoying this. Sheila directed the media presence, which was almost constant, to their designated zones. Doing nitty–gritty detail work wrapped in a light cotton camisole against the backward San Francisco summer with her long gray hair in a bun, and she, too, seemed to be enjoying herself. There were over a four thousand people at the rally today. A light day.

"They call it the *new way*!" Walcott's derision sounded doubly clear through the megaphone. "But what is new about the Tournament?"

"Nothing!" chanted the crowd.

"It's the same old war machine dressed up for the world to consume!"

The crowd cheered their agreement

"Its destruction brought to you by Capitalism, Incorporated!"

The crowd cheered louder.

"But we see through them! No matter how much lipstick you paint on this monstrosity, it's still state–sponsored blood sport, and people are dying."

The crowd applauded.

"Do you want to live in a world that worships its soldiers?"

"No! The match is at the wick! The match is at the wick!"

The chant rang across the park at twice the volume when the crowd caught whiff of Frank and Lock. Then it turned to a robust booing, echoing like the call of a massive conch shell.

Walcott stepped in with the megaphone. The Haighters were staunchly non–violent activists, in contrast to what they saw as the ultra–violence of the Tournament, but just to be safe, Walcott cut into the chorus of boos.

"These men aren't our enemies! They are deluded, but they do not represent the establishment we seek to topple! Save your deri-sion for those who deserve it!" He indicated to Frank and Lock that he would meet them to the side. He handed the megaphone to one of his lieutenants, a young, bare–chested man dressed in linen pirate pants who continued to speak. The crowd remarked Walcott's absence but for a moment.

Walcott made his way to Frank and Lock. Many handshakes

and back–pats later, he said, "I like the two of you, but you're crazy to show up here. Only most of us are pacifists."

"Heya, Doc," Frank said. "You look younger every day."

"I made a deal with God. I said, 'Don't kill me until I destroy this mess I created.' He said, 'Fair enough.' So here I am. Now the question is, why are you here?"

"We're here because we have it on good authority that, unless we do something quickly, you're about to light a bunch of candles," Lock said.

Walcott eyed both of them for a moment, brushing his worn suit free of the sprinklings of summer foliage. He turned back to catch Sheila's eye. He held up five fingers questioningly. She nodded and pointed to an area under a nearby tree that was free of media and protestors.

"C'mon." Walcott loped slowly over toward the tree. When they were out of hearing range of the multitudes, Walcott spoke again. "The yellow rose."

"You've heard of it."

"Everyone's heard of the yellow rose. To tell you the truth, there are a fair number of people in the crowd who support the movement, whatever it is. Anything to disrupt the system, they say."

"The man behind it is called the Gardner. He's not out to stop the Tournament, just to get rid of the people he doesn't like. Then, probably, to run amok with it as he sees fit."

"I figured it was too good to be true. I've seen a lot of would–be revolutionaries over the years, but the only person I've ever seen who wants to get rid of everything about the Tournament is the one standing right in front of you. It makes too much money for everyone else."

"I think he's gonna kill a lot of people," Frank said. "Including Ellie."

Walcott, about to go into one of his practiced tirades, stilled. Frank knew that, despite everything he said, Walcott would always have a soft spot for Ellie and Blue—the team he'd unwillingly brought into the Tournament by administering the polarization drug to each of them on a cold winter day in Cheyenne over a decade ago, opening their bodies to the damage a diode could inflict. But Ellie was no longer eighteen. She was a war-weary adult now, well beyond his influence.

"She plays in a game of death, Frank. You can't play in a game of death and expect to live long." He said it quietly, and his eyes were downcast. "She poisoned herself when she took the shot."

There it is again, thought Frank. *That word.*

"We spoke with him," Lock said, "with the Gardner. At gunpoint. He said the yellow rose would finish off the old teams because he had a poison pill with their names on it. Those were his exact words. Poison pill. Do you know what he could be talking about?"

Walcott pursed his lips then shook his head. "I mean, the whole thing is poison from the polarization inoculation to the diode to the booster, which only makes the players numb to their destruction. The weapon was designed to mimic a gunshot through vascular bruising, eventual numbing, and then full coma. It's all a poison. Ellie, all of them, they're walking poison pills."

"Yeah, but that's old news, Doc," Frank said. "We're talking something else. Anything else. Maybe an actual pill? Something he could move, get to teams across the globe? Something he could put into use right now to get rid of all the people who don't wear his stupid flower."

Walcott shook his head again. "They take a poison pill every time they get shot by that damned diode. It's just the way it is..." His face softened, and he blinked into the distance. "The diode..."

"Yeah, we get it, Baxter," Lock said. "The diode is poison. It's killing everyone. Capitalist war machine, yada, yada, yada—"

"No, the diode you know is a refined product," Walcott said. "Believe it or not, it's the best the development crew could come up with. You should have seen the early stuff. It absolutely wrecked the test subjects. Usually small mammals. It was death on contact."

"But you must have gotten rid of those early prototypes, right? Destroyed them?"

Walcott was silent.

"Right, Baxter?" Lock stepped forward.

It was already coming together for Frank. "No you didn't, did you."

"We went through hundreds of iterations," Walcott said. "Thousands and thousands of diodes. I don't doubt that some of the old models are out there, and if this man is as resourceful as you claim..."

"Where, Baxter?" Lock cut in. "Where could they be now? If he got them, he got them recently."

Walcott clenched his teeth and narrowed his eyes in thought. The sounds of chants called back and forth in the air around them. "If they're anywhere, they're in the Springs lab. But I haven't been there in twenty years. It may not even be operational anymore."

"Colorado Springs?"

"Yes, underground there. Bill Beauchamp, Sarah Foss, and I worked there for years."

"Abandoned?" Lock asked.

"Probably. All diode research is above ground now, at UCSD and at a major lab in Cupertino. Back then, almost nobody knew about what was going on."

"Can you tell us how to get there?" Frank asked.

Lock was already on the phone with their pilots.

*

The Colorado Springs Airport shared its runways with nearby Peterson Air Force Base. Frank and Lock's jet followed in the wake of a large military transport, dwarfed by their props as they navigated the tarmac before being shuffled off to the civilian hangers. After they rolled to a rest, the pilot opened the cabin door and turned to face them.

"We got about an hour here. I had to pull some strings with some Air Force buddies at the tower to even get clearance."

"Shouldn't be long." Frank popped off his seatbelt as he pulled his trusty notepad from his breast pocket. A set of explicit instructions was written there. If they followed all of them to the tee, they should be in and out of the facility and back in about an hour. They made their way down the stairway, which Frank always found far too steep, to a waiting rental, a cruising sedan.

From the airport, they drove west along Fountain Boulevard, following their GPS. To their right, a collection of monolithic stone formations stood starkly against the setting sun: the Garden of the Gods. To their left was a sprawling city center. Frank knew this town all too well. In his prior life, he'd lived not far from the Garden of the Gods in a sorry little duplex development on the far side of the shopping center by the car dealerships. His realtor had claimed he actually had a view of the state park, which was true only in an underhanded landlord sort of way. On a clear day, he could see the tip on one rock formation over the Applebee's across the street.

He and Lock had already been up for over twenty–four hours. Frank noted it distantly. He didn't feel tired. He rarely felt tired these days, especially when he and Lock found themselves on the chase. Something about the Tournament kept him, going. It was like the air in a casino.

"You all right?" Lock glanced at him. "You're pretty quiet. You're never quiet."

"I used to live here. Didn't much care for it. Guess I kind of have a case of bummer nostalgia. This is where it all started for me with the William Beauchamp life insurance claim all those years ago back at Barringer Insurance. Funny how things come full circle. Take a right."

Lock hooked right off the expressway onto a winding road that took them past the chain restaurants and outlet stores and deeper into a series of industrial warehouses with names that seemed to be pulled from the corporate hat: WorldTech, InterLogic, Global Next, and then, at the end of the road, Medical Logistics.

"There it is," Frank said.

They parked the car in an empty, six-space parking lot at the side of the building. Weeds and sun-bleached trash tracked the bottom of the wall. The steel door was marked "entrance" with faded paint. The lock was rusted. Frank stepped up to it and took out the key Walcott had given them, a standard door key he'd kept at the back of his key ring. He pushed it in the lock and turned while pulling the handle. No movement. He pulled harder, setting his feet. The door creaked, and a dusting of rust sifted from the upper hinge. But it pulled open.

"There we go. Step one is a success," Frank said.

Lock stepped inside the hallway. Emergency lights were on, but most had burned out, and those still alight flickered. He pulled a flashlight from the back pocket of his track jacket and clicked it on, sweeping the darkness. He paused when the beam illuminated the ground in front of them. There, faint but visible in the dust, was a series of footprints, leading in and going out. "Well, somebody was here recently. C'mon."

They made their way down the hall, following the beam and listening carefully for any sign of company, but the facility was near silent. As they made their way deeper, the hallway began to smell musty, of earth and wet metal. Another fifty steps, and they reached a single door elevator marked PRIVATE in red block lettering. There was a pad to the right. Frank tapped it, and it blinked to life. It read, *Place Thumb Here.*

"Here we go. Step two." Frank held his breath as Lock fished his handheld from his bag. He scrolled through it for a moment until he found the transplanted image of Walcott's thumb. He loaded it at high definition and pressed the screen flat against the pad. He shook his head, already prepared to get shut out. A light moved from the top of the screen to the bottom, like a scanner, and then beeped and turned green.

"Ha!" Frank hooted. "Step two! Success!"

Lock took the handheld back. The screen read, *B. Walcott: Approved.* The door slid open, but the elevator was completely dark.

"Yikes." Frank shied away, but Lock grabbed him as he walked past and pulled him inside.

"It'll work. The lights just burned out," Lock said. But as the doors closed and they were plunged into cave–like darkness, even Lock let out a breath. After a moment, the elevator jerked and descended. "See?"

"I can't *see* anything, Lock. How deep does this go?" Frank asked, his voice disembodied in the darkness.

"Walcott said a couple of hundred feet," Lock said. Frank heard him chewing at a nail. Just when Frank was sure even Lock was about to start sweating, the elevator jerked to a stop. The doors opened partway. Both men stared out at a dimly lit cavern beyond.

"Okaaaay," Frank said. "Guess I'll take it from here." He put his back against one door and pushed the other completely open with his feet. Lock ducked under his leg. Frank skipped out after him as the doors slammed closed. He glared at the doors then turned to take in the lab. It looked more like a cave than a lab, hollowed out from stone and wide enough to play a decent game of catch in. Only one part of it, the part in the far back, looked as though it had been used at one time. As they walked toward the silent equipment framed by three large drafting tables and a pair of desks, their footsteps echoed like the clapping of hands.

Papers were strewn all across the floor, and one rolling chair was tipped on its side in front of them. A computer on one of the three desks had turned itself on. A login screen read, *Welcome B. Walcott.* Below that, a cursor blinked in a box marked PASSWORD.

"This one's on too." Frank moved to another desk. He woke the computer up, and it read, *Welcome, S. Foss.* The third desk, the one Frank presumed belonged to the late Bill Beauchamp, was silent, the computer cold.

"The security system must turn the user's system on when they check in up top," Lock said. "So either S. Foss was here, or the Gardner used her prints to get in."

"I'm betting the latter," Frank said. "Sarah Foss was re-located to some research center in the boonies if I recall correctly. Hope he didn't cut her thumb off or anything like that. Look, there." He pointed at a storage closet set against the curved wall. Its front doors were ripped off their hinges. A crowbar lay on the ground in front. "Bingo."

The broken and bent doors were marked *Diode Specimens: 1–50.* On the shelves were rows of red boxes, each about the size of a handheld tool kit and marked WARNING: LETHAL DOSE. Frank picked out one marked TEST 50: FAILED TEST: LETHAL DOSE and popped the plastic clasps to open it. There, loaded in what looked like ten standard handgun clips, were bright red diodes.

"Well, shit," Frank said. "There's our poison pills."

"Shit's right," Lock said. "Especially since this closet is supposed to have fifty of these boxes full of diodes." Lock looked up and down the shelves. He counted ten boxes, including the one Frank held.

"That asshole took forty boxes full of one–and–you're–done diodes." Frank dropped his hands to his sides.

"I think we'd better make some phone calls. Quickly."

CHAPTER TWELVE

THE GARDNER FIT in remarkably well among the swath of tourists that swamped the Acropolis in Athens, Greece. He walked with a map held out in front of him, and a big sun-hat shaded his face. He stopped to tie his sneaker in front of the Old Temple of Athena. He liked Greece, but not because of the sights or the food or the people. He liked it because it served as a reminder to him of what happened when power was assumed. This very city was once the seat of world power, the wellspring of Western thought. The very tenets of discourse were brought forth here. Those who led from here assumed it would always be so. Now there was nothing but blunted statues.

Assume nothing. Change is powerful and constant. It'll get ya if you don't watch out for it, thought the Gardner as he snapped a photo.

The Greeks, Team Ivy, were gearing up for a Round Two matchup against Team Gold, the Italians, one of the original eight. The Gardner didn't like the Italians. To him, they were a boisterous and cocksure team of old–timers who refused to take his flower and refused to get out of his sandbox. Their captain,

Tessa Crocifissa, in particular, was a brash spitfire who thought herself above everything and everyone else. But for some reason, the Italian people loved her and her striker and sweeper. Gold had moved through the first round in style. Crocifissa, her eyes burning and her face set in a fierce snarl, had gunned down two members of their matchup herself, the newcomers from Vietnam who called themselves Team Oxen. The Gold wonks were still celebrating the win in the streets of Rome, drinking and chanting, draped in gold tinsel.

That really ticked off the Gardner.

He'd thought he'd given the Vietnamese plenty of help to beat Gold in the first round. He'd told them what type of formations Gold usually employed, who to watch out for. He'd told them to take down Crocifissa last. She was the most irrational. He'd even given the Vietnamese the exact time and place of their landing in Da Nang. All to no avail. And that had taken some work. He'd called every major news outlet and managed to swamp the airport where Gold wanted to land with media, which put their plane on divert from Hanoi and forced them to land in Da Nang in the first place. He'd handed them to Team Oxen on a gold platter, so to speak, and they still managed to screw it up. That was a problem because it meant that a team that had shunned him was still in the game.

The Gardner was tired of leaving anything, even the smallest thing, up to chance any longer. Time for a more direct approach.

When he walked in to the Ivy studios to the east of the Acropolis near the Greek Parliament, the doormen immediately gave way. He folded and set his brightly colored map in the trash as he walked up the marble stairway to their living quarters where one of them was still recovering from a diode wound sustained in the first round. He opened the outer gate and knocked politely upon the ivy–clad inner gate three times. When their captain, Stephanopoulos, who had taken to referring to himself in the third person, opened the gate, he blanched visibly.

"What, you're not happy to see me?" asked the Gardner.

"No, no, of course we are. Come in," he said, but the Gardner had already stepped past him and inside their war room.

A line of televisions spanned one wall of the room, each tuned to one of the major Tournament networks, all in a frenzy to recap the first round action. The Gardner noted with chagrin that they were still dancing and swaying in the streets of Italy. The opposite wall was an interactive map of the world, showing the teams and their statuses in updating dialogue boxes beside each country.

The Gardner stopped in front of the TV tuned to USTN, which had a live feed of the Cheyenne compound after Blue's loss. He smiled. That one had gone according to plan. He checked his watch and then looked back at the broadcast. The Cheyenne compound was quiet and sparsely lit. There had been some movement earlier but nothing out of the ordinary.

"What can Stephanopoulos help you with?" asked Stephanopoulos, close on the Gardner's heels.

"That went pretty well, didn't it? Your first round match against the Portuguese? Pretty sweet win, right?"

"Yes, Stephanopoulos and his team give their thanks. He wishes you to know that your information came in quite handy." Stephanopolous gave a stiff bow.

The Gardner cocked his head. "Cut it out right now. That's just silly."

Stephanopoulos puffed his chest out and brushed twice at his beard. "Stephanopoulos does what he—"

"Cut that shit out." The Gardner put his hands on his hips, his tone deadly serious. "Now."

The captain looked down, and his striker and sweeper were suddenly very interested in the Tournament feeds. "All right, I'm sorry."

"That's okay," the Gardner said, as if speaking to a child. "Now, you've got Italy next."

"We will crush them just like we crushed—"

"No, you won't," the Gardner interrupted. "They're better than you. At every position. It's a six tool team versus a three tool team. Four at best—only 'cause your striker is pretty good with a gun." He spoke not in admonishment, just stating a fact, but it left all three Greeks speechless. After a moment, the Gardner spoke again. "You'd be sunk if you had to get all three of them. But I do think you may have a shot at hitting one of them."

Stephanopoulos worked his mouth until the words came. "We will do more than just *hit* them. We will—"

"Shut up," the Gardner said flatly. He swung up his left hand, in which he carried a bright red plastic box by the handle. He plopped it down on the expansive marble island in the center of the room and popped it open. Inside were ten clips packed with bright red diodes.

"The only way you will win is if you use these diodes. So you will use these diodes. And then you will win." He clapped his hands once and then flipped them from palm to palm like a Vegas dealer chipping out at shift change.

The Greeks eyed them uncertainly.

"What are they?" Stephanopoulos asked.

"They're diodes. Newest model. Use them or die." The Gardner laughed. "I'm sorry. I meant lose. Use them or lose." He walked back to the USTN live feed of the Cheyenne compound. Snedeker and his panel were small boxed in the top right, discussing Blue's failure. He checked his watch again and then cracked his own neck luxuriously.

"All right," he said. "I gotta go. One more team to visit. Hey, keep an eye on that feed in about... four and a half minutes. You'll see yourself a show."

He walked past all of them, paused at the trashcan and pondered picking up his map again, decided against it, and walked out the door.

*

Stephanopoulos reached into the red box and pulled out a clip of red diodes. He popped one out. It looked the same as what they'd been using for years, aside from the color. He shrugged and tossed the clips to his teammates. He watched the USTN feed of the Cheyenne compound, turning up the audio.

Four and a half minutes later, with Snedeker mid–sentence, the main house of the compound exploded.

CHAPTER THIRTEEN

"DID YOUR PEOPLE get out?" Mazaryk asked Ellie, as she watched the explosion again and again on every feed, her face stony. Her house exploded with the force of a botched meth lab, throwing half of the roof against Tom's to the east and shattering every window in Cy's to the west. After a long pause in which Mazaryk didn't press, she answered him.

"Eddie, I was smart enough to beat you. You think I'd leave anyone on that compound after what you told me?"

Mazaryk pursed his lips into a small smile. Ellie turned to Cy, who watched the burning aftermath with cold, detached darkness.

"Is your family safe, Cyrus?" Mazaryk asked.

"Yes," Cy said. "They ran the tunnel right after us."

The tunnel was an underground escape route leading directly out onto the flood plane. They'd dug it and cemented it shortly after finishing the third house. It was the only private way in or out of the Cheyenne compound. Until Eddie used it the morning he visited, Ellie would have sworn nobody on earth but the three of them and Ian knew of its existence.

"They're with Troya's family," Cy said. "My house was empty. All of them were."

Mazaryk's jet banked left, soaring through the skies on its way to Europe. They'd been in the air for over an hour already, talking in the situation room. Team Black had a double–decker international airliner at their beck and call. The upstairs was turned into a situation room with live television feeds and an oval conference table. On the main level, where the first–class cabin would normally be, was the forward lounge. To the back of that were six individual sleeping cabins with queen–sized beds.

"That was my fucking roof he caved in. With your roof," Tom said, his face pale as he watched the replays.

Snedeker was beside himself with horrified excitement. "It's far too early to speculate" Snedeker said, right before speculating that Team Grey was most likely behind the attack as retribution for Auldborne's backbreaking loss all those years ago. "...a wholly unjustified bombing nonetheless. A brutal and ruthless attack that has all the hallmarks of a revenge hit. Tournament Medical and Security are combing the wreckage as we speak, looking for bodies."

"He's going to be quite disappointed when they find nothing but wood, brick, and old gossip rags in there." Ellie sneered at his face on TV.

"So, I suspect, will the Gardner," said Mazaryk.

"It was him, then?" asked Brander, sitting in a chair specially created for him, twice as large as every other around the table. His cane rested against the arm.

"I'm certain of it. Despite what Keith Snedeker may say, this has none of the hallmarks of Auldborne and Grey."

"You would know," Tom said. "You guys were best buddies for a while."

"My aim back then may have been misguided," Mazaryk said, locking eyes with Tom, "but I never doubted Alex Auldborne's commitment. He is cruel, but he's not a coward. If he were here now, he would call this cowardly." Mazaryk gestured at the televisions.

"Yeah, then he'd try to strangle us. While laughing," Tom added under his breath.

"It was the Gardner," Ellie said. "Alex wants to shoot us over and over again. The Gardner wants us dead for good."

"Hell of a way to kick off the second round," said Cy. "Talk about starting with a bang."

"I'm gonna turn in." Tom scratched his arm. He was pale again and sweating. He nodded briefly at Cy and Ellie before clearing his throat and standing. He seemed unsteady as he navigated the stairwell down to the cabins. Cy and Ellie exchanged a look.

"I need some time to think as well," Mazaryk said. "What perplexes me more than the fact that the Gardner tried to kill you by destroying you in such spectacular fashion is that Alex and Team Grey have yet to publicly deny their involvement. If you'll excuse me, I'll be in the forward lounge."

Mazaryk rose, and Ales and Brander followed.

"Get some sleep," Brander offered gently. "It'll keep you a step ahead." He nodded at the screen. "I'm glad you guys decided to come with us." He bent over to a near right angle as he descended.

When Cy and Ellie were alone, Cy turned to her. "Did Brander just tell us he likes us?"

Ellie smiled. "I guess he did."

"You know, ten years ago, that guy tried to throw a statue on me? And not a little garden gnome either. I'm talkin' a big–ass statue. And now, here he is telling me to get my sleep. I think I'm gonna have to write that one in my diary."

Ellie laughed, but her mind was on Tom.

"You want to check on him, or you want me to?" Cy asked.

"I'll do it." Ellie looked at her hands clasped on the table before her.

Cy let the quiet hum of the cabin envelope them for several seconds, then he nodded. "All right, I'm gonna go call Troya then." Cy stood. He looked as though he wanted to say more but decided against it and went down to his own cabin.

Ellie wanted to shut off all of the televisions, but she thought Eddie might object, so she simply stood and checked the countdown to Round Two before going down the stairs herself. *A little over twelve hours to go.* She remembered, back in the old days, when they'd given teams much longer to recover between rounds. The booster shot had changed all that. So had the constant network coverage. Even two or three days without action was too long for them. The people wanted gun fights.

Ellie fought back a roaring yawn. She was weary, made

doubly so by the soft white noise of the airplane in flight. She felt like she was asleep standing, and she thought how nice that would be if she had dreamed all of this, starting from Tom's overdose. She'd still have a house. They'd still be in Cheyenne with no death threats hanging over them. Maybe, if she was lucky, she'd fallen deeply asleep after she'd raised her fist in triumph at the Black House. Maybe everything since was a dream. *That would be nice.* But she knew it wasn't true. The Gardner was real. The yellow roses were real. And Tom had really almost died on her mere hours ago.

She knocked on his door, and for five cold seconds, there was no answer. Then Tom opened. His eyelids were heavy with tears, and he sniffled.

"I knew you'd come, but I couldn't help it," he whispered.

For half of a second, Ellie thought about slapping him in the face. Tom even prepared for it, shying away like a beaten dog. That was why she couldn't get angry. Instead, she sounded defeated right along with him. "God dammit, Tom." She shook her head and willed the tears back down inside her. She stepped inside the cabin and shut the door.

"I wish I could say you don't understand, but you do." Tom sank down on the bed. A small collapsible table to the right had nothing on it but a dusting of powdered heroin and a credit card. "You've been hit just like me. We don't feel the pain like we used to, but it's still there. In a lot of ways, it's worse. It's like it moved from our bodies to our souls. Only you can take it. I pussed out. I needed help."

Ellie sat next to him and put her head in her hands.

"Then it became something all its own. And now, here I am. Blowing dope in an airplane."

"How much more of that shit do you have, Tom?" Ellie asked hollowly.

"You're not gonna believe me, but that's it. I have more at home. I have a baggie full of the stuff. But I only brought the one bump for some reason. Sort of a last hurrah. Forced sobriety, maybe. I dunno."

She looked at him sitting beside her, his shoulders hunched, his face slack. She knew she should be furious at him, but all she wanted to do was hug him, hold him, let him know that he wasn't alone. "I believe you. Don't know why, but I do."

"You know what I always remember?" Tom still looked straight ahead at the closed door, his eyes blank. "It was this one day back in high school. Back in... forever ago. Everyone thought I was this confident kid. Lots of friends. Funny and all that. But you knew me from day one. You knew I was scared shitless about growing up. Everybody used to make fun of you, but you never let it get to you. You were the confident one."

"Tom, I was a mess in high school."

"Naw, you say that, but you always had your head on your shoulders. You remember that one day when you said to me, 'People watch what you do?' Remember that?" He turned to her, and his eyes were clear again.

Ellie did. It was the first time she'd ever really spoken to Tom Elrey. They were both eighteen then. Ellie nodded.

"I never forgot that. I think of that every day. Did you know that? I've thought of that every day since you said it. I remember exactly how you looked. This beautiful girl just chipped away at all of her life, but here she is standing there in front of me and telling me the first real goddamn thing anyone has ever said to me in my life."

Ellie felt herself flush, but Tom was looking away again and then at the ground. "More people than ever watch what I do these days," he said. "And more than ever, all I do is fuck up."

He turned and took Ellie's hand in his. "You think you're not worthy of all of this, but you couldn't be more wrong. I'm the one who shouldn't be here. You're the champion, Ellie. We could lose every Tournament from here until the end of time, and you'd still be a champion."

Ellie felt herself moving toward him, almost as if the plane had banked again, but it hadn't. She just wanted to be close to him, to press her cheek against his. But as she reached for him, the speaker dinged. It made them both pause.

Mazaryk's voice came over the intercom. "Ellie, Cyrus, Tom, I think you should join me in the forward lounge."

Ellie rubbed at her face, the spell broken.

Tom blinked, looked over at her, his ruddy face a new type of flushed. He rose and held out his hand. "Let's see what the czar wants this time."

Cy was already in the forward lounge, along with all of Black. They faced the far wall where a large television screen flickered with slight lag but showed Frank and Lock outside of what appeared to be an old strip mall. Lock was using his handheld to broadcast. The two were jammed close to each other in the frame like they were trying to take a selfie. Frank had cobwebbed debris stretched across his bald head.

"We're all here now, Allen. Go ahead."

"Thank God you're okay!" Frank cut in. "We were crapping ourselves over here! We just got out of this pit of death a hundred miles below the surface of the earth, and we hear your house has been blown up? Your freaking house was blown up?"

Lock elbowed him but nodded in agreement. "You had us terrified, Ellie."

"Yeah, well. Still alive. For now," Ellie said. "But thanks, guys. I know you're with us."

Frank held up a red box by the handle. He adjusted it to get it into frame, crowding out Lock, who took it in beleaguered stride. "We found something here that's a game changer. His game changer. The Gardner's."

Lock popped open the container and pulled out a clip of bright red diodes. Even in the satellite lag, they gleamed with poisonous malice. "We tried to warn the teams directly using the admin frequency, but either the Gardner's jamming the calls, or everyone is on lockdown for the second round and not taking incoming transmissions, so it's up to you guys. You gotta warn the remaining original teams, and you'd better warn them quick, 'cause we got a big problem here, guys."

Chapter Fourteen

EVERYONE IN ITALY wore masks.

In the early days of the Tournament, bandanas had been the most prolific way fans sported their team's colors: a simple kerchief in blue or black worn bandito style over the nose and mouth. Team Blue fans still wore blue bandanas, perhaps as a nod to their country's frontier past, but most of the other teams had evolved their own hallmarks. The Japanese wore the rising sun bandana. The Russian wonks and Black fans wore long black scarves (of wool or linen, depending on the time of year). Fans of Italy's Team Gold called themselves *Indorato*, "The Gilded," and they wore gold face masks reminiscent of the Italian renaissance. These ranged from cheap gold plastic to gold–plated leather, but it seemed as though everyone in Rome was wearing one as the final hour of the moratorium came to a close, including the six visitors who stepped off of Black's jet and were on their way to Tessa Crocifissa's five–story house just off the newly renamed *Plaza Indorato*.

Tessa was still a fierce fighter, but she'd taken less and less to traveling. She preferred to bring the spectacle to her. Mazaryk was betting that the Greeks knew this as well and that the action would unfold here, in Rome. The bells of the city rang in a thunderous peal as the moratorium expired. Black and Blue were stuck in a long, snaking line of traffic trying to get into the city. Their progress had halted altogether ten minutes earlier. People streamed in and out and between the cars, cheering and chanting, sliding over the hoods and slapping the car doors as they went. Black was in the front car, Blue in the back. Their windows were tinted. By now, the world knew that nobody was found in the rubble of the Cheyenne compound, but Ellie wasn't exactly keen to let the world know where she was just yet, nor with whom. The six of them wore full-faced golden masks in the style of the famous weeping bard that disguised them and let them blend in with the crowd.

The cars behind them honked to no avail. The cars ahead were pinned in for the foreseeable future. In their separate cars, the six of them watched the skies through the sunroofs and waited. Mazaryk had told them he still had contacts on the ground here. If either the Greeks or the Italians made a move, he would know, but it was the helicopters that tipped them off first. One minute, they were peppered about the sky in the distance, high enough so that their thumping propellers blended into the background noise. The next, all of them banked toward the Colosseum.

All six hopped out of the cars and onto the street as a wave of excited cheering swept over the city. "So much for those contacts. Eh, Eddie?" Tom said, but Mazaryk was already off, running along with the rest of the crowd toward the Colosseum near the center of the city. They'd been heading in that general direction from the airport when the traffic hit. They were close, but it would take some running, and everyone around them knew it as well.

The city's biggest tourist attraction on any given day was about to have its biggest crush in centuries.

*

Over the years, Tessa Crocifissa had grown lean and powerful in her hourglass frame. Her face was dark and freckled, and she hadn't cut her hair in almost a decade. She wrapped it around her head, and it splashed over her shoulders as she awaited Greece in the most ancient of battlegrounds. Beside her was her striker, Ignazio Andizzi, his trusty silver and gold guns out and at the ready, his linen pants flapping in the hot summer wind. Lorenzo Aldobrandi, her steely sweeper, made the third point of their triangle. They were behind a walled structure to one side of the Colosseum floor, part of a recreated staging area from where a gladiator might have emerged long ago. It was a clear challenge. Greece was to take the other side. This would be decided in the old way. The ancient way. The crowd streamed into the broken seats and spilled over onto the walkways. Gold masks clogged the open approaches, pushing toward the archways.

*

Blue and Black arrived as the crowd roared from the far end. Ellie strained her eyes to find the source of the uproar and saw a large black van pushing its way toward the main entrance. The driver was heedless of the crowd, maintaining a slow, relentless forward pace. The van was getting pelted with all manner of trash and debris but seemed to have been equipped for this. It moved forward like an armored slug, forcing the crowd away.

"That's them," Mazaryk said. "The Greeks."

"We'll never get to Gold in time," Ellie said. "They're almost at the entrance."

"If we don't, the Italians will die," Mazaryk said.

"I will distract," Brander said simply. "I'll draw the crowd to me if I can. Clear a way to the Colosseum floor."

Mazaryk nodded, then Brander stepped away into the crowd, using his cane both as support and as a stave. He already drew eyes for his height, but those nearest to him screamed when he removed his mask to reveal his long, narrow face, eyes wide and piercing, his mouth cut into a hawkish grin known the world over.

"Surprise!" He fired into the air with his gun and took off at a hitching gait, shoving the crowd out of his way.

A decade ago, perhaps more people would have run from a Tournament player than toward him. Times had changed. The wonks were out in force, for both sides, and they wanted their scars. A chunk of the crowd separated and took off after Brander, screaming wildly. The other five now had a small window and an even smaller sluice of an open path toward the Colosseum, and they took it.

The Greeks had a bigger path. Stephanopoulos and his men, dressed in dark blue fatigues, leapt from the van. They ran over the crowd and through the main gate, firing to clear their way. Ellie winced at each blast. She couldn't help looking for Cy and Tom, both grim beside her. All of them knew what even one hit from those guns would mean.

When the five of them made it to the inner lip of the

structure, Tessa was already striding out to meet the incoming Greek team, her gun low but at the ready and her teeth bright white against the worn rock around her. Ellie tried to scream a warning, but her voice was swallowed up in the thunderous applause that greeted Tessa's appearance. Team Ivy filed in and flattened themselves against the fallen stones of the west side of the circular battleground. They checked their clips and tapped their spares. Perhaps it was the wavy summer heat, but Ellie swore she saw a glint of red.

"There's no way we can get to them in time." Mazaryk spoke as if in a dream. His voice was muffled by his mask. Ellie pushed forward but was rebuffed by snarling fans. She watched in horror as Ignazio Andizzi, always the cockiest of the three, threw caution to the wind and charged in front of his captain, racing across the Colosseum grounds with deranged glee, firing at the Greeks on his way to cover on the south side.

He would never make it.

Stephanopoulos broke cover and shot at him three times. Twice, he missed entirely, but the third hit Ignazio Andizzi on the shoulder. He stumbled on the concrete and fell behind the ancient stone wreckage. The crowd roared in anger. Stephanopolous left himself open as he sighted Andizzi, and Tessa popped three diodes into his chest. She clearly thought she'd gotten the best of the trade as she ducked again, and the crowd did too. A shoulder wound for Andizzi in exchange for downing the Greek captain? A worthy sacrifice. Until she called for Andizzi.

Ellie could tell Tessa was screaming into her earpiece and that Andizzi, crumpled behind the ancient lodestones, was not answering her. Tessa turned to Aldobrandi, still at her back. He shook his head. The crowd was beginning to sense that something was wrong.

"We've gotta do something," Ellie said. "Eddie, can you get a shot at the Greeks?"

"No." Mazaryk sounded fascinated, almost entranced by the manner in which Ignazio had been snuffed out.

"Can anyone? Tom, Cy?"

"No, Ellie," Tom replied, his voice full or sorrow. "We're on the wrong side."

And indeed they were. They were on the wrong side to stop the Greeks and the right side to see the massacre of Italy. Ellie knew that the Gardner was here somewhere. She could feel him, smiling benevolently down upon them from behind one of these weeping masks. This man who was taking her Tournament from her. From all of them.

Ellie wasn't going to have it.

If she couldn't shoot the Greeks, she'd do what she had to do to keep the Italians alive. She beat her way forward through the crowd to the front line of the mezzanine. Tessa and Lorenzo Aldobrandi had their backs to her, about fifty feet in front of her and twenty feet down. Ellie pulled her gun from her shoulder holster, aimed at Tessa, and fired.

At first, the gunshots scattered only those nearest to Ellie, who ducked and scampered more out of surprise than fear. By her third shot, most of those around her were running for safety, but some grabbed for her. She ignored them, adjusting her aim quickly she fired a fourth time, and this one hit Tessa in the back, right at the upper spine. She collapsed in a heap. Ellie had just enough time to cover her face before the crowd overwhelmed her.

She was pummeled for only a moment. One man, a burly Italian in a T–shirt rolled up at the sleeves, pulled her mask off with one hand and raised his fist with the other until he recognized her face. He paused just long enough for Tom to brain him with the butt of his gun. Then Cy was there, throwing haymakers and clearing the crowd. Both of them picked her up by the shoulders, their own masks gone. The crowd stepped back in confusion. They knew who these three were, but they had lost in the first round. Yet here they were.

"Eddie!" Ellie screamed. "Take out Lorenzo before the Greeks can!"

Mazaryk glanced once at Ellie, ripped off his own mask, stepped to the retaining wall, sighted the only remaining Italian player, and fired once. His shot hit the sweeper in the head as he tended to his felled captain. Lorenzo collapsed beside Tessa, unconscious, but alive.

The crowd hesitated at Blue's surprise appearance, but they were staggered at seeing Black with Blue, both of them past champions. The clapping and chanting turned to screams of confusion.

"We've got to get out!" Ellie yelled. As if he'd been waiting for her scream, Goran Brander appeared by the main entrance. He fired his massive handgun three times to get their attention then waved them over. Mazaryk and Ales ran toward him. Team Blue followed. The crowd closed behind them and paused only a moment before pursuing, but it was enough for the six to make their getaway.

*

The rest of the Colosseum watched in confusion as the Tournament medics surrounded Ignazio Andizzi. The other fallen players had already passed the field check and were being lifted out of the Colosseum by winch and harness into hovering choppers, but Aldobrandi remained on the ground. The Greeks were not celebrating either. The remaining two stood around the medics as they worked on Andizzi, his white linen pants streaked with dust but still brightly fluttering in the wind as he jerked in measured time with the defibrillator. After several minutes, the medics stood. They stepped slowly away, and the silence of the circle, the slumped shoulders of each person there, told the crowd everything they needed to know.

Their beloved striker was dead.

CHAPTER FIFTEEN

WHEN THE CHEYENNE compound blew to pieces on live television, Ian Finn, along with the rest of the world, thought Ellie was dead. After the explosion, Ian had grabbed his phone, his hands shaking as they hadn't in years. A text from her number read, *We're chasing the Gardner,* saving him from a complete breakdown in Greer's office in the hills outside of San Francisco.

Brandt, who the team had disowned, at least temporarily, had no such reprieve and actually threw up on the office floor before Ian was able to calm him down and tell him Blue was alive.

Ian and Brandt were still going through files. Thousands of pages of Tournament paperwork had wicked every last ounce of moisture from their hands, which grew chapped and cracked, but still they hadn't found anything of note. Most of the files were dated dossiers of teams from past Tournament cycles. Several were jammed with spreadsheets containing row upon row of numbers that had no relation to anything Ian or Brandt could recognize. All of them were detailed and useless accounts of days gone by. One whole row was devoted to retired teams. The explosion in

Cheyenne lit a fire under them and kept them pressing on, but they had cleaned out almost every piece of paper in the office and had found no revelations of any sort.

"Nothing." Ian tossed another folder out of the office and into the hall, which looked like it had been hit by a tornado of busywork. "This stuff is all old. Why would he care about old stuff? It makes no sense to me." He rose from his chair and walked over to Greer's mini–bar, a stately mahogany piece set between the bay windows overlooking the hills. Ian had been drinking less these days. With Ellie, he didn't feel the need to drown himself nightly anymore, but he still loved a dram every now and then. And from the looks of it, Greer had been a connoisseur. Ian poured three fingers of rich amber and offered a silent toast to Greer before taking a healthy swig.

"I don't get it either." Brandt sat cross–legged on the floor surrounded by manila folders. He was still pale, and his hands shook slightly. "We keep the updated dossiers and team files at HQ in Palo Alto, but he didn't care about any of that. He said he wanted everything in this cabinet destroyed. This cabinet specifically."

Ian took his glass of whisky behind Greer's desk and sat down heavily in Greer's high–backed leather chair. He slumped. His phone buzzed in his pocket, and Brandt's rattled against the wooden floor at the same time. A Tournament update. Ian flicked his out of his pocket and glanced at it idly, expecting to see a text with some Round Two results. Instead, he got an update from Italy that churned his stomach.

Gold (Italy) loses to Ivy (Greece) at terrible cost. Colosseum showdown takes life of I. Andizzi (Str. Gold). Surprise appearance and quick exit by Black (Russia) and Blue (USA) fuels rumors of treachery.

Ian took a deep breath and downed the rest of the whisky.

"It's him," Brandt said, reading the same update on his phone. "The Gardner, he's behind all of it. I don't know how or why, but he is."

Ian massaged his temples, trying to think. What would a recruiter want in here that he couldn't get anywhere else? The man was high up on the Tournament totem. Recruiters probably had access to everything Greer had access to anyway. Except the Gardner didn't *want* whatever was here. He wanted it *destroyed*. So it was something he already had. Or knew Greer had. Something he wanted nobody else to see.

Ian tried to imagine Greer's final moments here. He'd probably sat in this chair. He might have had one last drink, just as Ian was having. Did he know he was going to die? Ian pictured himself as Greer, tried seeing the office through Greer's eyes. What did Greer know that the Gardner wanted wiped away?

Ian's eyes fell upon a picture, the only picture on Greer's desk, the only picture in the office, in fact. It was a candid picture of Ellie, Cy, and Tom from their promo shoot, probably between takes. They looked like schoolyard chums, leaning in against each other and laughing easily. Tom was cracking a joke that had the other two in stitches. They looked young. It must have been taken several years ago. Ian reached over and picked it up, fascinated. He noticed the picture itself wasn't set right in the frame. It was misaligned. He furrowed his brow. It bothered him that Greer would have only one picture and it would be offset like this.

Ian popped the frame open, and the picture fell out, face down on the table. There was writing on the back.

> *He is coming, and I do not think I will see you again. When John and Nikkie died and then Max, everything crumbled for me. You picked me back up. You put me back together. You gave me great joy again.*
>
> *Thank you.*

And then, below the note, Ian read a small inscription.

> *Underneath. To the left.*

Ian looked over at the cabinet. Then he looked to the left, at the base. The worked wood was slightly raised at the base between the feet of the cabinet. Ian walked over and kneeled there. Brandt watched as he reached between the cabinet legs.

"Unbelievable." Ian pressed the button he found there. A counterweight released inside the cabinet with a sharp rapping sound, and as it rolled, a panel eased out from flush with the side of the cabinet. Ian plucked it open with his fingertips. It concealed a small gap, barely six inches high, but it housed a thick stack of papers clasped together. The edges were worn, the paper yellowing. They looked well flipped through. On the top were written the words *Blue Sheets* and under that *Destroy After Reading*, an order that Greer had very obviously neglected to carry out.

"Blue Sheets?"

"The candidate lists." Brandt walked over to Ian. "Along with recruiter notes. I've never seen them in person. They aren't even supposed to be printed on paper. Once the recruiters settled on Ellie, Tom, and Cy, all copies were supposed to be deleted."

Ian flipped through the lists. There were hundreds of names. Hundreds of observations next to each name, each attributed to a recruiter. Ian scanned through until he found what he was looking for: Ellie Willmore. Next to her, a note: *3 Tool Candidate: Guts, Brains, Willpower. Superb observational skills. Disassociated from family. Loner. Friendless. Can be transplanted. Can be molded. Can be taught to win. Others will disagree, but I think she's perfect.*

And then next to that, the name of Ellie's recruiter: Eric Gardner.

"Holy shit," Ian said. "He isn't just a Blue recruiter. He recruited her personally."

"But that makes no sense. He's trying to kill her. He hires her, then he wants her dead?"

Ian tapped the papers on his forehead in thought. He took them to the desk and sat back down in Greer's chair. He checked the dates. The pages at the back were well over a decade old. The first sheaf was dated almost twenty years ago.

"There are recruiter notes from the first Blue team here too." Ian flipped the pages and scanned for *Northern*. He found him very near the back, on what was perhaps the most worn of all of the pages, adorned with coffee rings and marked with thumbprints. Ian felt a pang of sadness. He had fought against Northern but had always respected him. Another recruiter had marked a very brief note: *Close. Between JN and EG, but I think the choice is clear: JN.*

Below Northern's name, the recruiter had written the number 1 and circled it with a red pen. Ian flicked through the pages until he found the number 2. The recruiter note read: *Fearless and extremely bright, but not a leader.*

The name next to the note, the man Johnnie Northern had beaten out for captaincy of the first generation of Team Blue and who then went on to recruit for Blue, was Eric Gardner.

CHAPTER SIXTEEN

EDDIE MAZARYK WORKED three phones at once in the situation room of his jet, two mobile and one satellite. He spoke Italian in one, French in the other, and Russian in the third, moving seamlessly among conversations while watching the worldwide replay of Andizzi's death at the Colosseum.

He paused in his Russian conversation as Snedeker returned from a commercial break with his panel of ex–Tournament medical crew and Sarah Walcott, who were in a heated debate over what had happened to the Italian striker. There were thousands of camera angles, from cell phones in the Colosseum to cameras flying above in the media and medical helicopters. It was undeniable that Andizzi had been hit in the shoulder. Sarah Walcott argued that the hit was not even the type that would bring a quick coma, much less bring on complete cardiac arrest.

"Well, then what is your theory, Ms. Walcott?" Snedeker asked. "Are you suggesting foul play on behalf of Black and Blue, who inexplicably showed up right as Andizzi was killed?"

Sarah shook her head. She took a moment in which she seemed to visibly be calming herself in the face of Snedeker's comments. "That's not what I am saying at all, Keith, and you know it. I'm saying that this isn't what it looks like. We all know what a bad diode hit looks like, and that wasn't it."

"And yet Andizzi is dead. Gold was one of the original eight teams. Could it be that Andizzi was simply too old? Had been hit too many times?" Snedeker asked, a glimmer in his eye. He was spoiling for an on–air fracas. The other two panelists, as usual, voiced their agreement.

"Old?" Sarah replied, incredulous. "Andizzi was thirty–one, Keith. And a spitfire. He was healthy as a horse. There are plenty of people in this league who are banged up from one too many diode hits, but Andizzi wasn't one of them."

"And Blue and Black? How can we explain their involvement? They opened fire upon an active team. Were they working with the Greeks?" Snedeker removed his spectacles and peered at Sarah, who refused to back down.

"I agree that it certainly looks that way, but I think we must consider—" She was interrupted by the sputtering of the other members of the panel, who already considered her in Blue's pocket, but Sarah raised her voice over them. "I think we must consider that perhaps Blue were trying to get between the two teams. I think they know something about this yellow rose, and the Greek's involvement—" She was drowned out by a chorus of disparaging comments, including the incredulous laughter of Snedeker himself, who dismissed her with a wave of his hand.

*

Cy shook his head as Eddie muted the program, turning back to his conversation. "If Sarah doesn't watch it, she's gonna find herself out of a job."

Ellie pressed a compress to her cheek where she'd been clawed by the nails of a man in the crowd as he tried to take her down. "Then Snedeker will finally have his panel of robots."

Tom was at the bar, rearranging the bandage that spanned his chest. He'd wrenched his shoulder swinging at the man who'd scratched Ellie. He'd knocked the man cold, but he was fairly sure he'd dislocated something in the process.

"It's the perfect setup," Tom said. "The Gardner gets to kill off the teams he wants while making it look like it's our fault. Sarah Walcott can try all she wants, but nobody is gonna buy that we shot the Italians for their own good so the Greeks couldn't kill them first. Especially not with gasbags like Snedeker stoking every fire under our asses for ratings." Tom reached for the whisky. His hand twitched, and he eventually had to set the glass on the bar to pour.

Brander and Ales took the phones from Mazaryk, who turned to consult a digital map. Brander continued the conversation with whoever Mazaryk had on the other line while Ales pocketed his phone in silence. Tom slugged the rest of his drink. "What do you need a phone for, Ales? You checking emails on that thing, or what? Because you're obviously not talking into it."

"Just because Ales chooses not to speak doesn't mean that he can't, Mr. Elrey," Mazaryk said.

Ales looked plainly back at Tom.

"Well, the day I hear that man talk, I'll be able to die in peace," Tom said.

Mazaryk looked up from his map. "It is precisely his silence that has endeared him to a ring of contacts who have served us quite well over the years. The very same contacts who have just informed me that France will be making their stand in Strasbourg, on the border with Germany. It appears that their opponents, the Dutch, also received a recent visit from an American. Our contact said he carried a red box."

"So we're too late then. It'll be just like the Colosseum." Ellie gripped her armrests until her knuckles turned white. "I owe the French. They came to our side at the Battle of the Black House. They saved my ass."

Ellie saw Mazaryk disguise his chagrin. He knew all too well what the French had done to his city in that battle. They'd wreaked havoc and drew off his own contingent while Ellie made her stand against him. Mazaryk did not care for the French. But their antics were hardly the biggest threat facing the Tournament anymore.

"Allen was right about the direct lines to the players. Either the Gardner has blocked them, or the French are offline in order to prepare themselves. But Strasbourg is only two hours away. All is quiet on the ground thus far. Perhaps we will arrive in time." Mazaryk went back to his map.

In the awkward silence that followed, Tom took a big breath. "Well, we've got the French at death's door without them knowing it. We've got a crazy American dealing golden bullets to the teams he likes with one hand and trying to kill us with the other. We've got the networks saying everything is somehow our fault, and now I hear that Ales Radomir actually can talk, even if he chooses not to. I think I'm gonna go lie down for a bit."

As Tom left the room, Cy and Ellie traded a glance. After another moment of watching the muted television in the humming quiet, Ellie stood and followed. Mazaryk nodded to her. She thought it particularly good of Mazaryk that he never questioned or even broached the subject of what he'd seen when he first met them at the compound with Tom on the floor. She wondered if perhaps he had some familiarity with masking the pain and the pressure of the Tournament with substances.

This time, Ellie didn't even need to knock on the door. Tom had left it open for her. As she stepped in his cabin, he was still fiddling with his chest dressing. She closed the door behind her.

"I wasn't lying to you about not having any more dope." Tom sat down on his bed and winced. "I would never lie to you."

"If you did have more, would you use it?"

Tom looked up at her, his washed blue eyes tinged with red. He nodded. "Probably." He looked at his shoulder, and his face soured. "I think it's dislocated. It's not torn. I've torn it before. Dislocated it too. This feels more like a dislocated shoulder."

Ellie held out her hands. "Get up. We'll pop it back in. You know the drill."

Tom blanched, but he let her help him up. He slipped himself sideways in her arms, his shoulder pressed flush with her breastbone. She wrapped her arms around him.

"On three, ready?"

He bit his lower lip, and she could see his heart hammering through the vein on his neck, but he nodded.

"One, two, three." She pulled him hard to her and felt the shoulder shift under her chest, snapping back into place. He groaned through his teeth, sweat sprang from his forehead, and he sagged against her. She held him for a minute.

"Is the pain really that bad?" She whispered into his ear.

He turned toward her, his face inches from hers. "It's bad, but you have old war wounds too. The pain is only part of it."

"What's the rest?" Ellie found that her voice was small and scared, and her heart hammered too. She felt the color rising in her face, betraying her again, just like always.

"You. Loving you and knowing you're beyond my reach and always have been."

Ellie knew. She supposed she'd always known. That Tom admitted it to her now, finally, was less of a revelation to her than a sad, strange portent. He'd kept it to himself for over a decade. Confessing told Ellie that he felt he was at a crossroads, a turning point, maybe even the end of things. And it was that sense of impending loss—of a change in the winds—that kept her there, with her arms around him, when even a month ago she most likely would have disentangled herself. She saw that Tom knew it too, and with the quiet desperation he leaned toward her and kissed her. And she kissed him back.

They pressed each other to the bed, and when Tom winced again, Ellie held her breath because she found that she didn't want anything to derail this moment. "Are you okay?" she whispered, and he nodded. She folded his arm sling–style over his chest as he settled on his back, and then Ellie very quietly undressed herself. She even took care to stifle her belt buckle as she slipped out of her jeans. Tom watched her with longing as she undressed him as well, but she left his shirt on and set her left hand gently on his shoulder as she climbed on top of him. She kept her left hand there as she kissed him, only taking it away to guide him inside her. Her hand returned to his shoulder, cupping it softly as they pushed against each other so that she remembered where it was and not to grab it or pull it or lean on it. They were completely silent, even at the end. Only their breath could be heard in the cabin along with a rhythmic pressing, not much louder than the squeezing and releasing of a fist.

In the blank seconds afterward they watched each other. Ellie swallowed, working moisture back into her mouth, and Tom smiled in a carefree way that Ellie hadn't seen since high school. Neither spoke because they knew that if they did, their pocket of peace would be broken, and the reality of what they had done would come crashing down upon them.

*

Ellie's phone rang from inside her jeans, which were set carefully over the chair, and the peace was broken for them. Ellie climbed off of Tom, found her balance again, and found her phone. It was Ian Finn calling. She answered.

Tom knew by her tone who she was speaking with. He watched her carefully as Ian asked if she was okay, his voice small but audible in the cabin. He'd seen the footage at the Colosseum. It struck Tom that Ian never once questioned her motives or told her to stay out of danger. He knew what type of woman she was. He trusted her. Ellie put the phone on speaker as Ian told her about what he'd found in the hidden drawer in Greer's office.

"Two things," Ian said. "The first is that this Eric Gardner became a recruiter only after he was passed over for captain. Northern beat him out."

Ellie ran her hands through her hair and wandered over to sit back on the bed, close to where Tom still lay, half naked. Tom was afraid to move even an inch.

"The second thing…" Ian paused, as if he'd second-guessed telling her for a moment.

"What's the second thing, Ian?" Ellie asked clearly.

"He's not just any recruiter. He recruited you."

For Ellie, everything seemed to stop. It was as if the airplane was being held there, suspended in the air, neither falling nor moving forward. Even her breathing stopped. All of the questions she'd asked Greer about *why* she'd received her commission and *how* it could be that she was chosen over the rest of the country crashed together in her head like a cacophony of cymbals. The loudest of them all was the tacit implication that the man who had hired her now wanted her dead.

Ian seemed to hear the noises in her head because he spoke again, and his tone was one of talking her back from a ledge.

"Ellie, I know your mind is racing, but don't read anything into this without the facts. We don't have them yet."

Ellie closed her eyes. "We know that he's the reason I'm here. We know that he wants us gone."

"Not just you." Ian's voice was careful, his intonation clear. "He wants a lot of people gone. This is a big purge. It's not like he's on a crusade against you alone. And we're all with you."

Ellie came back to the present. She thought of the French. She thought about Andizzi, never to be revived again. She took a deep breath. Ian was right. In his quiet way, he'd reminded her that this wasn't about her. This was bigger than her.

"Ellie, are you okay?"

"Yeah. Thanks, Ian. For all the digging."

"I'm coming to you," Ian said. "If this guy is anywhere near you, you're gonna need all the help you can get to take him down."

"No." Ellie shook her head, and her gaze landed on Tom. Her heartbeat ticked faster. "You're one diode away from death, Ian."

"With the Gardner running wild out there, so are you," Ian said, softly chiding. And, of course, he was right. They were all one diode from death now.

"I'll find you. I love you," Ian said.

Ellie broke eye contact with Tom before she said, "I love you too."

Tom seemed to sag a little more into the bed, his eyes closing. Ellie hung up. Tom was still, eyes closed, while Ellie dressed. Ellie walked over to him and kissed him lightly on the forehead. There was nothing in this kiss of the kisses before.

"We're about to land," she whispered to him. "Are you still with me?"

"Always."

CHAPTER SEVENTEEN

STRASBOURG, FRANCE WAS a city of old cobblestones and high–banked canals. During the day, the old town along the River Ill, called *Petite–France*, was a thoroughfare of tourists and Gothic architecture buffs. The night belonged to the cafes and the cats that roamed around them, eyes glowing in the moonlight.

"She's a strong city," Yves Noel said. "Look, even the cobblestones are as thick as a man's arm. She can take a firefight. Plus, if things go really badly, it's close enough to Germany that maybe we can push the shitstorm east into their country." He winked and raised a glass of wine to Ellie, to Mazaryk, and to his own joke.

Black and Blue had no trouble finding the French Triplets who made up Team Silver. They rarely made a secret of where they were these days. They also had a longstanding tradition of radio silence and moderate to heavy drinking before any fight, which meant they were usually to be found in the local bars, pubs, and clubs. This had been true when they were twenty–five and back when they'd come to the aid of Blue against the Black

House, and it was true now, when they were closer to forty than thirty. They'd lost neither their rakish charm nor their trademark style, living as one unit. These days, they wore seersucker, their hair shined with product and parted with the edge of a knife.

"That's what we're saying, Yves." Ellie tried to make him understand. The busker's walk outside their cafe, already crowded with Silver supporters, was now swollen as news of Black and Blue's arrival spread. People were in danger of falling into the river. Yves seemed to sense the panic in Ellie's voice, and the quiet presence of Eddie Mazaryk and company had clearly bothered him from the start. His glass of wine hung in the air.

"I take it, then, that this is no social call. I should have assumed as much when I heard the two of you were padding around together."

"What is the problem this time?" Dominique, the Silver striker, asked. "Because last time, if you'll recall, Edward, it was a hostile takeover on *your* part that brought Blue and Silver together."

Mazaryk stepped over to Dominique and leaned down toward him. "As long as the Tournament exists, someone will try to rule it. This time, it is the yellow rose. The difference is that I wanted you alive. Eric Gardner wishes very much the opposite."

"We were offered the yellow rose by this Gardner you speak of," Tristan, the Silver sweeper, replied. "We turned him down."

"We are in business for ourselves," Yves said. "Always have been."

"That's why he wants you dead." Tom sat back in the shadows. His appearance had sparked a shrill outpouring of cries from the women in the crowd that he seemed in no way in the mood for at the moment.

"This man doesn't ask twice." Cy sat next to Tom, propping him up in more ways than one. "Andizzi found that out the hard way in Italy."

"That was the Gardner's doing?" Yves asked.

Ellie nodded vigorously. "He's gotten his hands on old model diodes. Lethal doses. One nick, and it's game over for you. For all of us."

"And he's given them to the Dutch, although we believe they don't know what they have. Nonetheless, they will use them against you."

Yves slowly brought his glass to his lips, looking back and forth between Ellie and Mazaryk as he downed his wine in big gulps.

"Well then." He wiped his lips gingerly with a white cloth napkin. "That settles it. We're retiring."

Mazaryk let out a sharp exhale. Ellie waited for the joke, but Yves wasn't smiling. Outside, the crowd grew louder by the second. Everyone who might have been sleeping within *Petit–France* was now no doubt wide awake.

"You think I'm kidding?" Yves asked. He looked to his brothers for confirmation. They shrugged, finishing their own drinks. "We make too much fucking money to get killed by some flower–wearing Dutchmen. Right, men?" He stood and took up his coat. His brothers followed suit.

"If you ask me," Dominique said, "this Tournament went

way downhill after Black House anyway." He winked at Ellie and adjusted his cuffs under his jacket.

"What's the good of being famous if you're dead?" Tristan asked.

"Tell this Gardner he can shower the whole fucking world in roses for all we care. I didn't get into this game to die for good," said Yves.

Goran Brander, leaning low over his cane at the windowsill to watch the gathering crowds outside, let out a low rumbling of Russian. Mazaryk moved to the window, spoke briefly with Brander, then turned back to Yves.

"Too late," Mazaryk said.

What Ellie at first took to be an overflow of people falling from the streets into the canals quickly showed itself to be much more direct. It was as if a massive rabbit burrowed under the crowd of people at the water's edge, flinging bodies into the water like clumps of displaced dirt. As the shockwave rolled toward the cafe, Ellie caught a flash of bright orange, the color of the Dutch.

People pressed in every direction. Cries of fear mixed seamlessly with chants of support from the Silver and Orange sides. In the cafe, the triplets backed away from the window. Blue and Black also pressed to the back of the building. Cy joined Ales and Brander in flipping the tables against the window for cover. Wine goblets popped like light bulbs.

"Well, shit, guess we're un–retiring." Yves tried to smile, but his voice bobbled in his throat.

"You could always fall on your own sword," Mazaryk said.

"Or we could shoot you ourselves. You'd be in a coma, but you'd come out of it at least. You'd avoid the fight."

Yves spat. "We're opportunists, Edward. Not cowards."

"There are nine of us," Tom said. "We're quite good at what we do. We can't take out three of them? They're a new team! We have two champions here," Tom held out his hands. "Can't you see? This is exactly what he wants to show the world: that the old guard is terrified of the new guard."

"We can get around them if we hurry," Ellie said. "They're following the river bank. We can pen them in on three sides, force them to set down the guns or jump into the river."

The other players hesitated. The windows rattled. "We've got to move now if we're going to move," Ellie said, her voice tight. Mazaryk nodded.

"My team will get behind them," Mazaryk said. "Silver gets in front of them. Ellie, you press from the side toward the water."

With Tom and Cy behind her, Ellie ran out of the side of the cafe, her gun out. Yves and Mazaryk faced each other. "Grow old on your own terms, Yves." Mazaryk's eyes sparkled with anticipation. He whistled at his team, and they left through the service entrance in the back.

*

"All right, my brothers," Yves said when only the three of them left. "I always say this, but now I really mean it. Don't. Get. Shot."

With his words hanging in the air, he shot out the front

window of the cafe and stepped around the strewn tables, and the Noel triplets went forth to confront the Dutch.

*

For the first time in his Tournament career, Eddie Mazaryk was thankful for the crush of people surrounding him as he led Black in a loop around the outer edge of the waterfront. Brander was his vanguard, the human equivalent of the front plate of a locomotive, and with Ales behind him, quick as a cat, Mazaryk was never in danger of being overrun by fans. They simply surrounded him, and in this case, provided a barrier between him and the red diodes in the Dutch guns. What Mazaryk found most difficult was the cell–phone intrusion. Fans, wonks, and even those caught up in the moment would dart in, snap a picture of him, and dart away. Black's progress was like the cyclists climbing the Pyrenees during the Tour de France. They had a single rivulet of space, nothing more.

By the time Black was able to loop behind the Dutch, the French triplets were already in Dutch sights. Silver had walked right toward the Dutch with the freedom of movement that often came with the home court advantage. The three teams were lined up from left to right on the bank of the River Ill: France to the left, Orange in the center, and Black behind them. The river promenade was clearing as Black finished their loop. Fans jockeyed for position, most of them fleeing the path, a few pushing toward it, looking for their chance to be an accessory to the news. The scene was reminiscent of a holy festival with clumps of people parading around a select few as if they were holding relics aloft.

Mazaryk was still hemmed in, and he thought of the time,

years ago, when he would have simply shot his way through this crowd. He saw the Dutch positioning themselves against the French. He saw that the Noel triplets were exposed, cringing in the open, knowing what was at stake, and yet still standing. Two thoughts occurred to him. The first was that perhaps he had misjudged the French all these years. The second, the one that came to him as he found himself unable to deal out the collateral damage he needed to get to the Dutch before they could open fire on the French, was that perhaps it was time for him to retire. In Mazaryk's mind, the moment you were unwilling to do whatever it took to get your man was the moment you needed to step down. This realization hit him not as a mark of weakness or with the sting of failure, but more like the subtle brightening after a passing cloud. He was not built for this competition anymore. Once Gardner was dealt with, he would hang up his guns.

But Gardner wasn't dealt with yet. If he couldn't shoot the Dutch, Mazaryk could at least make some noise. As the captain of the Dutch aimed at Yves Noel, Mazaryk and Ales and Brander each unloaded a clip into the air. They sounded a loud challenge, like a match tossed on a mound of explosives, and it was enough to get the attention of the Orange. The three Dutch flipped their aim, sighting the sound of gunfire, and the French took advantage. Yves fired into them, his gunshots echoing across the water. The crowd roared with each shot and doubly so when one of the Orange went down, collapsing to his knees and favoring his right hip. Mazaryk almost had a clear line. He nodded at his team to take any shot at will just as the Dutch opened fire.

*

Yves thought he'd mastered his fear of death. He'd come to

believe, over all of the years of drinking, shooting, carousing, and money–making, that he'd put all fears of death behind him. He'd accomplished more—lived more—than any one man could rightly hope to. But when the Dutch captain, a slight man in a tight orange shirt who Yves had no doubt was not intending to kill him but who would kill him nonetheless, aimed at him, all of Yves's convictions left him.

"Get down!" he screamed, and he and his brothers dropped to the floor. Yves felt the wind of one diode as the Dutch returned fire. They were pinned between two teams and unable to set themselves, so their first volley went high. Two more diodes screamed by Yves's head, and he was certain the next would kill one of them, but the Blue showed up.

*

Where Black fought the crowd, Blue had blended into it, taking a page out of Fethi's guerilla tactics handbook. Ellie, Tom, and Cy snaked through the crowd like water over the rocks. They wore full Blue bandanas to hide their faces as they made their way toward the canal. The Dutch had been bookended, and it was up to Ellie to either get them to throw down their guns or to push them in the river.

Cy broke through the crowd first. He got four shots off, three of them on target. The Dutch sweeper fell to the ground feet from the striker. Only one member of Orange was still standing: the captain. Cy took no chances with his own life, which he considered to be tied up with three others now, not including Ellie and Tom. After his hits, he faded back into the crowd, allowing them to swallow him up with their screaming and grabbing, but he misjudged their voracity. He found himself pulled back by the fans, being taken away from the field when he meant only to find some brief cover. He fought against the current of people like a drowning swimmer, to no avail.

*

Tom Elrey and Ellie Willmore found themselves out in the open, flush against the remaining Dutch, with nothing between them to blunt the deadly diode the Orange captain fired their way.

For Tom, it was as if this diode was fired from the barrel of a gun years ago, and it had traveled at an impossibly slow pace, millimeters a day, but on a direct path.

The day he'd met Ellie, the day she talked to him in the halls of Shawnee, that diode was fired. Over the years, he'd walked around it, to the left and to the right, above it and below it as he'd lived his life. But all the while, the diode kept coming. All the booze, women, and drugs, none of them would slow that diode. He knew this now. It was a gunshot that had taken a decade to hit its target.

And that target was Ellie.

In his mind, Tom went through the aftermath of their time in his airplane cabin, the aftermath that never was but that he understood nonetheless. He saw Ellie sitting down with him, telling him how what had happened between them was something they'd both needed, She'd say she did love him, but in the way that they both loved the Tournament, in the way that one warrior loves the person who stands beside her as they storm the beaches together. It's love, but it's not *the* love. And she could never give him *the* love.

She could only give that to one man: Ian Finn. Tom knew that Ian had done what Tom couldn't do. He'd gotten out, and he'd done it for Ellie. Tom couldn't get out. For the very same reasons

Ian got out of the game, Tom had to stay in, and it was all for this moment. This gunshot. This diode. And rather than curse Ian's name or curse his own lot as Max Haulden had done before him, Tom found a split second of eternity that gave him the peace he'd longed for. It fell upon him with the knowledge that no matter what Ian did, no matter how long the two of them lived together, and may it be long and happy and fruitful, Ian wasn't here now.

Tom was.

Tom jumped in front of Ellie and took the red diode to the chest. Tom's life went up in a plume of acrid gun smoke to the sound of a roaring crowd. He felt no pain, no slow bleed, only a surging rush of adrenaline pushed too far, not unlike the overdose he'd had in his kitchen. It was as if the cells in his body were boiling over, snuffing the flame below the pot. He fell lifeless to the ground in front of Ellie.

*

The Dutch captain didn't get off another shot. The crowd finally broke before Mazaryk, and he sighted the man and dropped him seconds after Tom fell, but the damage was done. Of the four who fell that day, the three Dutch and Tom Elrey, only the Dutch would ever rise again.

*

Ian Finn saw it happen. Another three hours and he might have been able to see it in person, but as it was, he had the best seat in the house watching on the airplane television. He could almost feel the strained silence as Ellie looked down at her feet, at Tom lying there, her arms out, poised to catch him but empty. She was frozen like that, as if she'd dropped a precious piece of crystal she'd been carrying.

The roar of the crowd was immense, even through the television speakers. Snedeker's play–by–play was completely drowned out. But then the frenzied cheers, the French chants of victory, all of them slowly died out as the medics hit the field, and what happened in the Colosseum was repeated in horrible clarity by the River Ill. The Dutch comas were confirmed, and they were lifted from the battleground, but something was wrong with Tom Elrey.

Again and again the medics pricked him with shots, pumped his chest with compressions, and revved the defibrillator. The medics screamed at each other and the crowd to back up and then backed up themselves. By then, it was so quiet on the cobblestone streets that Ian could hear the water scraping against the canal walls on its way to the ocean.

Ian saw Ellie drop to her knees, cradle Tom, and then kiss him deeply. When he still didn't move, she began screaming. She screamed wildly even as she bowed her forehead to Tom's, pulling his lifeless body up by the lapels as his head lolled. She screamed until Cy had to pull her up and away by the waist. Ian saw in her eyes and in her pain that she had loved Tom, and he knew that they had been together.

Ian also saw an American tourist in the first row of the crowd. He wore cargo shorts, sandals, and a t–shirt that read I ♥ BLU. His ball cap was perched high on his head, and it pushed his hair out over his ears. Under its brim, he smiled broadly at his handiwork.

Chapter Eighteen

THERE WAS A little known fact about Keith Snedeker, chief anchor of USTN, the most watched man in the world, the man whose professional guarantee was that his viewers would stay ahead of the players: he didn't care about the Tournament. All that Keith cared about was air time, and he knew that the most effective way to get in front of the camera and in front of millions was the Tournament. It was a means to an end for him. So he felt no remorse at Tom's death. Quite the opposite. When it happened, live on air, as he was giving the shot–by–shot commentary, his stomach dropped out not in sorrow or pain, but in anticipation—anticipation of the firestorm to follow, of the endless topics he now had for his panelists. Of the ratings. The sweet, sweet ratings. The only thing that would have been better was if Ellie herself had died.

He was in his dressing room at USTN Studios in New York City, watching the battle at the River Ill recap that he'd just finished narrating and preparing for his *Tournament in the Round* panel show. He had two story lines to hammer. The first was that it was clear now that the older teams were breaking down.

First Andizzi, now Elrey. The second was that, for the first time in Tournament history, two teams who were beaten in the first round had made a reappearance in the second. In the Tournament world where there were no such things as rules, the term *cheating* was never used. But certainly it was warranted here? The old teams were weak, and they were cheaters. That was tonight's theme. That ought to drum up enough outrage on every side of the coin to keep his show well ahead of every other in the ratings.

One assistant was polishing Snedeker's spectacles, and the other was lightly patting his face free of any oils that the broadcast lights might pick up, when there was a knock on his dressing room door.

"Enter." He said, shuffling his personal notes. He wanted to find the perfect question for Sarah Walcott to embarrass herself with. He hadn't yet publicly spoken of her dalliance with John Northern all those years ago. Might he drop a subtle hint? Insinuate that she'd always been unabashedly in Blue's pocket? It was a little underhanded, but now was the time to pull out all the stops.

His producer, a demure young lady who Snedeker thought had quite a lot of on-air potential—perhaps too much, and so he had "promoted" her to a spot directly under his thumb—entered and stood behind his chair.

"You'll never guess who just waltzed into the green room."

For a second, Keith held his breath. The Gardner? "Who?"

"Frank Youngsmith and Allen Lockton. They have some sort of exclusive info for you. They say they want to go on the panel tonight."

Snedeker smiled widely, and his makeup artist took the opportunity to dust his cheeks. He loved exclusives, especially when they came to him and not the other way around. Youngsmith and Lock were two more unabashed Blues, but he had no doubt he could handle them. He controlled the panel, after all.

"Run it out on the line that we have an exclusive with these two jokers. Tell them we're on air in thirty minutes," Snedeker said while visions of ratings danced in his head.

*

As the intro to *Tournament in the Round* rolled, Snedeker looked across the table at Frank and Lock like a jackal. He sat in the center of the frame with his handpicked contributors to his left. To his right, Sarah Walcott took a deep drink from her glass of water and nodded encouragement to Frank and Lock, who sat beside her. Lock was slightly green, his coloring offset badly by the shine of his tracksuit, which the lights picked up severely. Frank was in a rumpled suit and tie and sweating profusely. On the table in front of them was a red plastic case.

The cameraman started the countdown then passed it to Snedeker. In an instant, his vulpine stare was gone, replaced by the congenial half smile and earnest, engaging demeanor the world trusted for Tournament news.

"Welcome back to USTN's nightly *Tournament in the Round*, where we help you to stay ahead of the players. We have a lot to get to tonight, chiefly, of course, a panelist discussion in the wake of a second devastating loss this cycle, the death of Tom Elrey, Blue's sweeper and the charismatic face of the team for over a decade. What happened? And where do we go from here?"

The camera angles switched, and the red light jumped from the front rig to the side rig. All of the panelists switched in time except for Frank and Lock, who were left staring into space for several moments until Snedeker's producer could get their attention. Sarah helped with a quick clearing of her throat.

"As always, with me are Dr. Adam Eichler, former Tournament physician, and David Woo, ex–Tournament medic, along with Sarah Walcott, spokesperson for the Walcott family and a Tournament insider herself. We have two special guests on the panel this evening to help us tackle the day's events: Allen Lockton, chief of the Tournament Courier Network, and Frank Youngsmith of *The Youngsmith Report* fame and now a Tournament courier himself. Welcome, gentlemen."

Lock swallowed and gave a hard nod. Frank waved briefly at the camera.

"Let's get down to business. We've lost another brave warrior today, the second in as many days. What can we draw from these deaths? Doctor Eichler?"

Adam Eichler settled his shoulders and folded his hands before him. "The elephant in the room here is that both of these men, Andizzi and now Tom Elrey, are from the old generation of teams. They were both at the Battle of the Black House over a decade ago. These men were old in Tournament years, and diode hits are known to build up over time."

Snedeker nodded beneficently. "So what you're saying is these last diode hits might have been the straw that broke the camel's back. David?"

David Woo leaned in and cleared his throat. "I have personally revived Andizzi, Keith. Let me tell you, it isn't pretty.

He—and I'm sure Tom Elrey is the same—they've taken big hits. The real tragedy here is that they both were too proud to recognize that they needed to step down long ago. Before it cost them their lives."

Keith nodded, "Harsh words, but perhaps this is a time for harsh words. Sarah, your family has crusaded against the diode for some time. Your father would be the first to agree with Doctor Eichler and Mr. Woo, would he not?"

Sarah narrowed her eyes for a split second, trying to judge Snedeker's aim in these questions. She felt he was leading her, as he often did, into some trap.

"Of course Baxter has warned for years about the dangers of the diode, but I think he, and I, and all of us, ought to take a really close look at the circumstances in which these deaths occurred. Every other reported case of diode–related death has come after the player was successfully revived, when they simply couldn't fully recover. These two men dropped dead from shots that should only have wounded them, at worst—"

Lock held up a shaky finger and made a tentative attempt to insert himself into the conversation before being cut off.

"Ms. Walcott is right," Snedeker said. "We ought to look closely at the circumstances. In both cases, Team Blue appeared out of the blue, as it were, and involved themselves in a battle that wasn't theirs. I mean, let's face it. Blue was out. So was Black. And yet they refused to accept it. To many, it seems quite underhanded. Does it not?"

Eichler and Woo nodded in agreement.

"Underhanded?" Lock blurted. "You have no idea what's going on here. Do you?"

Snedeker laughed along with his panelists "We realize that you, Lock, along with Frank, are involved with Blue. Ms. Walcott as well. Intimately so."

"What's that supposed to mean?" Sarah straightened in her seat.

"Just that the three of you should have some clear insight into the culture of—let's put it frankly—of *failure* that Blue has adopted of late, that has led to the tragic death of Tom Elrey. Their defeat was hard enough for the American people to swallow without also piling on this bizarre post–exit tour that they are on. Mr. Youngsmith, your investigative work made you famous in *The Youngsmith Report*. What do you make of this?"

Frank looked from Snedeker back to the camera as if resisting an extreme urge to pick at his nose. He wiped his forehead with the sleeve of his jacket. The silence lingered.

Snedeker chuckled "We're all a bit speechless, aren't we? It's an embarrassing situation."

"You're definitely not speechless," Frank said, stilling Snedeker mid–beat. His eyes flashed in anger. "All you do is talk, Keith. You're definitely not speechless, but you are wrong."

"Oh?" Keith asked. "What about?"

"Pretty much everything," Lock chimed in. "Andizzi and Elrey didn't die. They weren't foregone casualties of the Tournament. They weren't old. They weren't washed up. They were killed by these." Lock popped open the red case and took out a sleeve of red diodes.

"What are we looking at here?" Snedeker asked.

"These are early model diodes," Lock said. "A man named Eric Gardner gave them to the Greeks and the Dutch to use against Gold and Silver. They kill on contact. Blue and Black were only trying to warn them. To save them. There was nothing underhanded about it. They risked their lives to save those teams."

Lock waited for the collective gasp of understanding from the panel, but it never came. Sarah took a sleeve of the diodes and studied them carefully.

Snedeker's face was long and skeptical. "You're telling me that this is all one big conspiracy."

"Yes, the yellow roses, the explosion at the Cheyenne compound, the deaths of Andizzi and Elrey and of Greer Nichols, all of it was orchestrated by a man named Eric Gardner, a past recruiter for Blue. A Tournament insider," Lock said, his voice shrill and cracking.

"Please, Lock, we don't do sensationalism here. The yellow rose movement is nothing but a symbol for the young teams to rally behind. It represents growth. It's a fun anecdote, nothing more. And we've been over the Cheyenne explosion on this show before. Alex Auldborne has all but admitted it was his doing."

"He's admitted nothing." Sarah still eyed the diodes as she spoke. She carefully popped one from the clip. She looked at Frank, who nodded at her.

"That's the point. He refuses to deny allegations. He knows nothing can be pinned on him. He's always been one for spectacle. It was him, not some Gardner fellow who cultivates yellow roses." Snedeker chuckled. "I recognize that you want your team—your friends—to be remembered in a good light upon their exit. And this is almost certainly their exit, one would have to believe. But I'm afraid they lingered a bit too long."

"How long have you been working for him?" Frank asked quietly.

"I'm sorry?" Snedeker replied.

"I said, how long have you been working for Gardner?"

"If this man exists, I've never seen him in my life—" Snedeker spoke with just the right amount of affront.

"That rose," Frank continued, thinking aloud. "That rose that came out of the Countdown Box on live television. That was meant for you. You took it, didn't you? What did he offer you to be his mouthpiece, Keith? Insider info? Exclusive access to teams? I bet you didn't come cheap."

Snedeker shook his head sadly. "Gentlemen, I've been more than gracious, but I have to put an end to this. The only people I work for are the American people and anyone around the world who wants honest, fair Tournament coverage." Snedeker took off his glasses. "We're the most trusted name in the Tournament for a reason. We get there first because we're the best." He turned to the cameras. "More after these messages."

*

When the red lights on the cameras blinked off, Sarah got up immediately, excusing herself. Snedeker watched her go and sighed with contentment as the makeup artists touched him up.

"Perfect, it really is. Yellow rose conspiracy? The man's name is actually *Gardner*? I mean, c'mon, boys. That's a little rich even for me. This public meltdown of Team Blue just keeps getting better. You make my job easy. Now, if you'll excuse me, I need to use the boys' room before we get back to this fabulous train wreck. Don't go anywhere."

Snedeker got up and walked quickly off stage. He was fully confident that his viewers would see Frank and Lock for the crazies they appeared to be, but it was better to be safe than sorry. He didn't get to the top of his game by leaving loose ends. He rounded the corner to his dressing room, taking out his key to unlock the door, only to find it already open. He froze. He took a deep breath then smoothed his jacket and walked inside. There, by the door, stood his producer.

"Sarah said you needed something." She eyed him quizzically. "You should be at your desk, Keith. We're back in three minutes."

But Keith wasn't paying attention to his producer. He was watching to Sarah Walcott, who stood by his mirror with the vanity cabinet open. In her hand, she held a glittering yellow rose.

"Frank was right. You're in his pocket. You've been working for him the whole time."

Keith Snedeker confessed nothing. He neither broke down nor became incensed. Keith Snedeker had never lost his composure a day in his life, and he wasn't going to start now. He cleared his throat, stepped up to Sarah, and plucked the rose from her hand.

"Nothing but a bauble. Your friends are fools. The rose is a symbol of the future. If you want to stay alive in this game,

Sarah, you've got to learn to side with the future. The past is too easily forgotten. Now get out of my dressing room."

*

Alex Auldborne watched the exchange between Frank, Lock, and Snedeker live from the third floor of his Hyde Park estate with his balcony windows open to the London summer night. A soft, steady breeze ruffled the curtains. The sounds of the city were a muted hum. He had a chilled glass of scotch in one hand, and the other rested on his gun. He was flanked on one side by Tate, his ever-present striker, fierce, loyal, unquestioning. Christina Stoke sat at his other, a china doll with a badger's attitude, absolutely devoted to him. Together, the three of them had easily survived to the third round—cakewalked, really. And with Gardner's help, Auldborne knew the remaining rounds should prove just as easily won.

He should have been comfortable. He should have been content. He was well on his way to his first championship. But he wasn't comfortable. He itched. He threw the stately covering off of his legs and took a deep sip of scotch, but it did nothing to calm him. This itch was more than skin deep. He scratched at his neck and chewed at his lip as *Tournament in the Round* came back from commercial break, and he saw Youngsmith and Lockton, two American apologists he detested along with Sarah Walcott, but who were nonetheless right on the money the entire time with their red-diode revelation, get shut down by Snedeker and his lackeys. They seemed defeated like two brownnosers telling on the school bully, only to be reprimanded themselves because nobody liked a snitch. Sarah, in particular, looked defeated. The other two were more in shock, but she looked lost, which was ironic because they were right about Snedeker.

Snedeker was most definitely in Eric Gardner's pay. Everyone who wanted to win was, including Auldborne. His next match was against the Germans, a team Auldborne had thought possessed of the good sense to go along with the yellow rose, but who apparently thought themselves above it. There was a time when Auldborne himself would have thought similarly, but then life came and dropped him out of a window. Ten years passed, and now he found himself with one last shot. *If you want to win bad enough, you can't be above anything.*

He took out his revolver and snapped open the round chamber, spinning it with a flick. It buzzed in the quiet of the room. Tate and Stoke looked up from their own ruminations. He loosed the chambers, and six red diodes tumbled into his lap. Gardner knew that Auldborne's shot was second to none. *"This is how you win,"* he'd said. And it was true.

Tate and Stoke watched him sift idly through the diodes like a diviner looking for answers in the tealeaves. They had become quiet of late, and the unasked question Auldborne knew was on their lips was *Do we want to win like this?*

He knew this because the same question plagued him. That was the itch, and with each passing day, it became harder to dismiss.

When Eric Gardner had told Auldborne that all he needed to do to win was stay quiet, he didn't think it would entail having the entire world judge him guilty of destroying the Cheyenne compound like a firebombing fanatic, heedless of the innocent family that might have been inside—of Troya Parker, now Troya

Bell, and her child. The entire world was so quick to agree that he had done it and was capable of doing it. That started the itch. It was one thing to act like a monster and be called one fairly. It was another thing to simply be assumed to be the monster.

The worst part of all of it was that Auldborne had come to realize the bombing was not something he would ever have done. It was the height of irony, he thought, that when he finally found the line he wouldn't cross, the world assumed he'd jumped right over it.

If he'd spoken then, gone in front of the cameras and cleared his name, perhaps it would have ended everything, but he hadn't. Instead, he'd gone on to fight and win. Now he was beholden to the Gardner. He plucked up one red diode. Here, in his hand, was his ticket to glory. At the Gardner's insistence, he had already let it be known that he would be awaiting the Germans on neutral ground at a special location, a place that still haunted him with the way it had thrown his life off track. The Gardner convinced him that there was a curse there, at that place, a curse he would break with a win over the Germans. A win that would cement his ascendancy but would also almost certainly mean the deaths of his opponents and perhaps others as well.

In a game without rules, they courted death constantly. It was part of the allure. That was what he kept telling himself. But more and more, it was wearing thin, itching.

He plucked the dried rose, exposed now without his blanket, from its place in the side of his chair. He felt a strong desire to crush it. He even looked at Tate and Stoke, who in their silence were essentially giving assent. But he was in too deep. He picked up the diodes again. It was his misfortune to know he was dealing death, but in the end, his choices were the same. Play with the Gardner and win, or fade away forever.

Auldborne slammed his fist against his legs. He felt nothing. If only the rest of him could feel the same.

*

Since the explosion, an army of wonks had cleaned and removed what remained of Ellie's house. The idea was to rebuild there, but after Tom's death, the place where her house had stood became a place of open solitude. Tom's house, in the back of the compound, became a shrine. The fences surrounding the compound no longer stood. People wept in the open dirt and placed tokens of remembrance along the path to Tom's house. The walkway leading to his door was a river of flowers that Cy had to pick up and set aside as he and Ellie, aided by Eddie Mazaryk, and with Brander and Ales at the rear, carried the pine box holding Tom's body inside. The crowd seemed to sense the grief coming from Ellie and Cy as if it were a physical wave holding them at bay. Other than the soft cries escaping from the crowd, all that could be heard was the *thunk* of single-stemmed roses as they hit the coffin and the sweeping sound of Cy moving them out from underfoot.

Ellie sat by the coffin for an entire day, until Tom was taken away from her for his autopsy and eventual cremation. She no longer cared about the Tournament, no longer cared that the second round was nearly finished and the third round would soon be upon them. The Gardner would almost certainly strike again, but she'd lost too much already. Her team, her friend, a man she'd loved. She fell into an exhausted sleep in Tom's bed, and when she awoke she found his pillow damp with tears under her head.

The autopsy report came back listing massive internal bleeding as the cause of death. Ellie didn't care. She already knew what had killed him. It wasn't just the diode; it was also her. He'd died for her. He'd died because he loved her, and when she turned away from him after their night together, he'd loved her regardless.

When Cy came back with the urn, he placed it where the coffin had been, and Ellie wept on his shoulder. She felt weak but couldn't eat. She felt tired but could no longer sleep. They sat together in the living room of Tom's house and told stories of their years together. The only time she felt she wouldn't be ill was when she talked about Tom with Cy, so they talked a lot.

They talked for a full day with Troya and Maddie coming in and out, leaving food and drinks and sometimes listening. When Ellie broke down, Maddie would put her small hands around Ellie's calloused, scarred hand, and Cy would hold her until her sobs no longer shook her. For five days, Ellie disappeared inside herself. She lost nearly ten pounds. She felt that if it weren't for Cy, Troya, and little Maddie, she might have wasted away to nothing.

On the sixth day, she was visited again by Eddie Mazaryk, Goran Brander, and Ales Radomir. Ellie knew they had walked Tom home with her, but in her grief haze, she couldn't remember when or how they had departed. She'd assumed they had left her and Cy to their defeat. They walked into Tom's house and stood exactly as they had when they'd found them tending to Tom as he lay at death's door on the floor with blood running from his nose. Ellie was so disjointed that she actually caught herself looking at the spot at the foot of the refrigerator, and when she found it empty the ache returned. She'd saved him then, but she couldn't save him for long.

Mazaryk paused as Ellie, Cy, and Troya looked up at him. He brushed at the smooth skin of his chin and seemed to be carefully considering his choice of words. "I won't say that Tom gave his life for this and that you should fight on because of it because it's quite clear that Tom didn't give his life to keep the Tournament out of the hands of Eric Gardner. He gave his life to save yours. He gave it for you. It seems callous of me to ask for you to risk it again on behalf of the Tournament, but I'm here doing it all the same. Eric Gardner is still out there, and he needs to be stopped."

"He's already taken everything from me," Ellie said. "My team is broken. Our generation is over. We'll never see another draw or another cycle. All I risk now is my life and Cy's life. Let Gardner take the Tournament."

Mazaryk watched her for a moment and then walked in and sat down on the couch. He steepled his fingers and rested them between his knees. "You don't know what you're saying. I do. I know what will happen when one man controls the Tournament, when one man pulls all the strings and controls all of the capital. I know because I was almost that man. But then you made me realize that I would be destroying what I loved. Everything I'd worked for, everything my father worked for, would become a charade.

"That was ten years ago. Back then the Tournament was just a tool. It settled scores. Now, it rests in the hearts of the people. When Eric Gardner controls the Tournament, he will control much more than power and money. He will control the people who love this game. It will all be his. Everything. To do with as he sees fit."

"Then go, Eddie," Ellie said, not daring to meet his eyes. "Go and stop him. Your team is healthy. You have a chance."

"No, I don't. Not without you. We're symbols, you and I. We're not just champions, we're champions who overcame the rift I split through the Tournament with the Black House."

Mazaryk sighed and slumped a little, and Ellie saw for just a flash of a second an old man in his visage. A tired man. "This is my last fight, too," he said. "I know it. I've lost a step. More than a step. It's true. Individually, we're old teams. But together we are the old guard, a symbol of what this Tournament was founded on, what it was, and what it can be again. The world's greatest game. The purest form of competition. It's not meant for any one man. It's meant for all of us."

In the silence that followed, Mazaryk stood. In a rare show of affection, he grasped Ellie on the shoulder briefly before signaling his team to the door.

"There's still one more of the old guard left," Mazaryk said. "Alex Auldborne and Grey. He's made it known that they will fight tonight against Germany. In twelve hours. The battleground he's chosen, or more likely that the Gardner has chosen for him, is a direct challenge to you and to me. He means to bury us where the first generation of Blue was buried: at the old shipping docks in Chula Vista."

He left it at that, stepping from the room and out of the house without another word. Ellie, needing to be alone with her thoughts, stood numbly and walked into Tom's room. She fell upon his bed with Mazaryk's words ringing in her head, and she slept the sleep of the grievously wounded, although her wounds were in her soul. Her body basically shut down, and she might have slept through the day and the night and made her decision to go to Chula Vista or to stay in Cheyenne a moot point, were it not for a second visitor who awoke her two hours later, with ten still to go before Auldborne's fight.

*

Ian Finn's trip proved shorter than he'd expected. He saw Tom Elrey die when he was in the skies over the eastern seaboard. He knew that they'd be taking his body home to Cheyenne, so instead of meeting Ellie in France, he told his pilots to change course. He touched down in Wyoming and made his way to the flood plain. The tunnel access still stood: a nondescript metal door set inside one wall of the concrete spillway.

He walked the tunnel and almost turned at the passage to Ellie's house until he was reminded by a mound of dirt and collapsed concrete that it no longer stood. Instead, he took the far path, the one that led to Tom Elrey's house. That was how he found Ellie sleeping in Tom's bed.

Not wanting to startle her, Ian brushed her arm lightly with his fingertip. She stirred, and he moved away from her to sit in a chair in the corner. He watched as Ellie found herself again, blinked, and focused on him.

*

Ellie held her breath. She checked the time then turned back to him. She couldn't tell what he was thinking. He'd hunched over himself in the way that he used to, back before they were together.

"How did you get in?" Ellie asked, her voice scratchy.

"Cy let me in. Took the tunnel. I think I was spotted at the door, but I don't care if anyone sees us anymore." There was no reproach in Ian's voice, but Ellie wondered if he meant he didn't care because he wanted everyone to know or because there was no "us" anymore. She knew what he'd seen on television. Ian was perhaps the most perceptive man she'd ever known.

"I slept with him, Ian." She said it not only because it would be insulting to Ian not to acknowledge the fact when it hung over them like a shroud but also because she felt that if she hid it from him forever, it would be another part of Tom that was buried, and far too much of him was already in the ground. Ian nodded. He knew.

"I did it for him. I did it because he was my right arm, and he was in pain. I loved him because he was a part of me. I miss him like a phantom limb. Not like I love you. Not like I would miss you, if you leave me forever too. Does that make sense?"

Ian, who had lost a teammate as well long ago, a fiery young woman named Kayla MacQuillan, knew very well what it was like to love and lose in that way. He nodded again, but he said nothing.

"But what I did, it wasn't worthy of you. Nothing changes that. Not then, not ever, not even now that Tom's gone," Ellie said.

"Would you do it again?" Ian asked quietly.

Ellie paused. She had deceived him once. She wouldn't lie to him again. "I don't know."

Ian let out a shuddering breath.

"Are we over, you and I?" Ellie asked in a teary whisper.

"I don't know."

"Is that why you came? To tell me you don't know what to do with me? Because that makes two of us."

"I think you know what you need to do, Ellie. You've got to finish this. You've never been a quitter. That's why I fell in love with you. You never quit. You're not quitting now. I think you're just preparing."

"Preparing? For what?"

"For Chula Vista. To finish this at Chula Vista. All you needed was me to tell you that you didn't kill Tom Elrey, no matter how much you want to pile this on yourself. That's your guilt talking. Eric Gardner killed Tom Elrey. Now he's called you out. You and Mazaryk. I know you won't back down."

Ellie flopped her head back onto the pillow. She knew Ian was right. She knew she would be meeting Mazaryk, who probably sat patiently right now in the forward cabin of his jet at the airport, less than an hour away because he knew it, too.

"Don't do it because of what I say, and don't do it for Greer or Tom. Do it for you. Do it because Eric Gardner is a bully. A big one, but a bully nonetheless, and you've never taken well to being bullied."

Ian rose. He didn't walk over to her or kiss her goodbye. He didn't even grasp her hands or hug her. All he said was, "The world will be watching." Then he left her. She sat on the bed for another minute then went into the bathroom. She took a cold shower and scrubbed the tears and the sleep and the grief from her face and then stared at herself in the mirror. She saw her scar, a lumpy, muted pink line that ran down her face and pinched the corner of her mouth. It was further proof that Ian and Mazaryk were right. They'd all fought too hard to hand the Tournament over to any one person, much less a complete lunatic like Eric Gardner.

Things were unfinished, and Ellie hated leaving things unfinished.

She dressed herself, wrapping a blue bandana loosely around her neck. She grabbed her gun and walked out into the main room, where she found Cy sleeping on the floor with Troya asleep on the couch. Maddie was stretched out on Cy's stomach, her thumb in her mouth, her eyes closed.

Ellie walked quietly to the door. Cy would hate her for it, she knew. He might never forgive her. That was fine. He had his happiness. He'd earned it. Ellie would never place another one of her family in danger again. If she lived through this, she'd gladly add him to the list of people she'd be apologizing to for the rest of her life, right next to Ian. It didn't matter so long as he was alive.

Ellie stepped out the door and closed it softly behind her. If Cy and his family heard the noise of the mourning crowd, they either thought nothing of it or had become so used to it that it was the background of their dreams. By the time they awoke hours later and realized that they were the only three left in the house, Ellie and Team Black would already be in Chula Vista.

CHAPTER NINETEEN

BEFORE JOHNNIE NORTHERN and Nikkie Hix died there, the lower Chula Vista docks hadn't been much more than a desolate strip of derelict buildings. Many of them were actively falling down, inching toward the ground month by month, exposing their steel framing and rusted loading equipment like the metal guts of ancient, dying beasts. They remained that way for a time after the deaths, but when *The Youngsmith Report* came out, and more and more people learned about the Tournament, the docks changed.

Where Northern and Hix had died, just off the wooden running dock, where the trash–strewn water surged back and forth against the concrete pylons, a monument had been erected. Because the first generation of Team Blue had been cut short before anyone knew about the Tournament, Hix and Northern were largely unknown as individuals. They would remain that way. Northern had no known parents, and Hix's family in Tennessee were private people who preferred to be left alone. What was known was their symbol, the mark of Blue: a teardrop shape that looked like a drop of water one way and a gout of flame the other. It had been on their right shoulders, tattooed in rich, black ink. Max Haulden, who had betrayed them, also had the mark.

The Blue wonks wanted to remember the team while avoiding the hard history between Haulden and Northern and Hix, so they'd recreated the first mark of Blue in copper and steel and set it on one of the concrete pylons just out in the water. The sun burned off the steel for fire, and the copper slowly oxidized for water. It became a pilgrimage spot of sorts for the Tournament faithful and had been cleaned up accordingly.

The way Ellie, Mazaryk, Brander, and Ales approached the docks was very different from the way Auldborne had that day, over a decade ago, when his team was set to face Northern and company, who had entrenched themselves in a large, abandoned shipping building. For one, the six of them had been alone on that long ago night. There hadn't been a soul around for many blocks. Now the perimeter was brightly lit, the air dotted with helicopters tracing spotlights through the sky, and the docks were jammed with people. The infamous shipping building had been turned into a museum and souvenir shop.

Ellie noted with an ache in her heart that a second, makeshift memorial had been erected on a pylon to the right of the first memorial. Someone must have swum out to reach it. She recognized her own mark, the second mark of Blue—three even columns—fashioned quickly out of metal and bolted to the concrete. A pinpoint spotlight shone from the dock onto one of the three columns. The one on the right, the sweeper's position, was illuminated for Tom Elrey. As she passed it and the crowd moved around her, she gave a nod, pressed her hand against her chest over her heart where the mark was inked, and threw a fist out across the water toward the memorial. The crowd, unsure at first how to react to the four of them, burst into roaring applause.

Before they reached the wooden dock, Mazaryk stopped and turned to Brander and Ales.

"This is where our path stops, my friends. Only Ellie and I will be going on from here. You have your orders. You interfere only to remove my body."

Fat tears dripped from Brander's face, falling upon Mazaryk's shoulders as Brander dropped his cane and bent to embrace his captain. "Calm yourself, Goran." Mazaryk smiled. "I'm not dead yet."

He turned to Ales, and Ellie was surprised to hear the silent sweeper speak, in quiet Russian. Mazaryk listened carefully then embraced him as well, kissing him on both cheeks. Mazaryk stepped away and turned, and he and Ellie continued their walk toward the heart of the lower docks, where the museum stood.

"What did he say to you?" Ellie asked.

"He said, 'See you on the other side.'" Mazaryk replied. "Ales, for all of his silence, knows what to say when it counts. No matter what happens here, it is the end of a great many things."

"And the beginning of a great many more? Just trying to keep this from looking like a funeral march."

Mazaryk laughed, something Ellie had only heard a handful of times, which was a shame because it was a beautiful laugh, like a child's.

"Perhaps," Mazaryk said. "We shall see."

The crowd pulled in behind them as they walked, rounding the bay along the dock until they came within sight of the museum. It was lit by spotlights and blanketed with the thumping sound of helicopters above, but the people had been moved away. The place stood like a quarantined building, stark and bright against the dark sky. In the ocean beyond, boats floated near and far like lanterns.

Mazaryk paused to take it in. "I must admit, I never thought I'd see this place again. The first time I was here, I tried to warn John Northern about Max Haulden. I was too late. Now, it appears we may be early."

The crowd packed the far edge of the dock, across from the water, but there was no sign of Auldborne or the Germans and no gunfire to be heard.

"Good. Maybe we can stop Auldborne from killing anybody." Ellie pulled her gun out. Mazaryk followed suit.

"It could be that Eric Gardner gave the Germans red diodes to use against Auldborne. Or perhaps both teams will have them. The Germans refused the rose, but Grey is a first–generation team. I believe Gardner wants both teams out. Permanently." Mazaryk tucked his tie in and buttoned his black jacket with one hand.

"Wonderful," Ellie replied flatly. "That asshole's giving them out like candy."

"Your instinct will be to target Auldborne. I understand this, given your history. But I ask you to wait until you absolutely must. I know the man better than you do. I may be able to reason with him. Remember, if everyone here ends up dead, Gardner wins. We must expose him somehow."

"You really think he's here?"

"I know it. He's been spotted at every battle involving the old teams. He's here." Mazaryk panned the crowd. "But we'll have to draw him out."

Ellie and Mazaryk approached the museum with caution. The crowd roared around them, darting in and out of the cordon, but they seemed to understand that the pair was to be left alone. The crowd noise jumped an octave as they stopped in front of the doors. Ellie looked at Mazaryk. They both knew what that meant. Somebody, or some team, was already inside.

Ellie took a breath and opened the big glass door. Mazaryk swung in, his gun up. Ellie followed him inside. The crowd surged around the building, but none entered. When the glass door closed, the sound was muted somewhat, although strangely dissonant, as if it came from damaged speakers.

The shipping building–turned–museum still utilized all of the interior architecture of the old building, reinforcing it here and there but maintaining the look of the place on the night Blue and Grey last fought there. The front doors funneled visitors between two concrete walls into the main space. Across from the doors, on the far side, the back wall had a second level, an exposed walkway where Johnnie Northern had helped Nikkie Hix drop to the ground so they could make their escape. Northern had shot out the skylight, and the two of them ran for the exit through a shower of falling glass. The skylight had since been replaced with stained glass that split and colored the helicopter spotlights like a prism.

The main floor had been turned into a spacious walking exhibit presenting a detailed timeline of Blue from as far back as the wonks could accurately figure, around five years before Northern's and Hix's death, all the way up to the present. Ellie's championship at the Black House featured prominently under the stained glass. Her career since snaked toward the back, which, she felt, was entirely appropriate. The far back, where Hix and Northern had been pressed during their firefight, was now a gift shop.

As they entered, they were presented with a projector screen showcasing a welcome video, complete with clips and narration of Blue's high points and low points. It ran on a loop. The smooth, professional voice of the narrator sounded odd and out of place in the emptiness. But of course, it wasn't empty, not completely. Ellie felt it. They were being watched.

"Alex!" Ellie called out, and then, considering the Germans might be there first, she called out the Amber captain as well, "Astrid?"

Silence.

"You're being used." Ellie's voice echoed. "You're fighting to the death, and you're doing it for a man named Eric Gardner, whether you believe it or not."

"Oh, I believe it," came the reply, followed by a soft hum, like the cruising of an electric car. In the back, on the raised main floor by the gift shop, Alex Auldborne glided out from behind the exhibit showcasing Blue's worst years. He wore a grey suit of light cotton, its collar and lapel so sharp they stood on their own, framing his neck and head. That the past decade had been as much of a struggle for Auldborne as it had for Ellie was written plainly on his face in shadows and lines, but he'd never aged out of his posh bearing. That was ingrained in the way he carried his chin an inch higher than everyone else and the way his brow seemed to arch a degree more severely. His trusty chrome revolver lay comfortably on his lap on a paisley throw that shimmered in the lights. "Quite the museum, this is," Auldborne said. "Can't say I care for the middle exhibit, but I especially like the last bit here."

"Alex." Mazaryk stepped forward and, Ellie couldn't help noticing, slightly in front of her own person as if to shield her. He spoke to Auldborne like an old friend. "Whatever he's offered you, it's not worth the price."

"You don't know what he's offered me, Edward." A brittle smile played on Auldborne's lips.

"A championship," Ellie said. "That's what he promised you, isn't it? That you'd win it all?"

"Among other things," Auldborne said. "Hello, Ellie." His voice dripped with vitriol. "I've been thinking about you a lot lately. You and your boyfriend. You have left your mark on me. It's time I repaid the favor."

"Alex, I've gone mark for mark with Ms. Willmore. It doesn't give near the satisfaction you're thinking it will."

"Shut up, Edward, you fucking hypocrite. The only reason you're here right now is because you failed where Eric Gardner has succeeded. And you have the balls to stand here and lecture *me*? This isn't even your fight, and yet you two are here. You *lost*. You're *out*. But you continue to parade about in the spotlight because you can't get enough of it." In a flash, Auldborne's gun was up.

Ellie raised her own gun, but Mazaryk stilled her hand,

practically pushing it down again. He needn't have bothered. As soon as Ellie saw Draden Tate and Christina Stoke out of either end of her peripheral vision, she knew they were on the wrong end of a standoff. Ellie froze, not daring to move.

"Put your guns down." Auldborne glided toward them. "Both of you. Now."

Ellie had never wanted to say *I told you so* more in her life. If she wasn't terrified that the slightest untoward movement might kill her, she would have. As it was, she set her gun to the ground an inch at a time as did Mazaryk.

"You're making a mistake, Alex," Mazaryk said. "We're not your enemies."

Alex rolled to a stop several feet from them, his gun in hand and resting comfortably in the crook of his chair, like that of an Old West poker player. "You keep saying that. But you're wrong. This one had her boyfriend break my back. What the fuck does that make us, exactly? Friends?"

Ellie grit her teeth. She knew better to antagonize Auldborne. He was the type of man to shoot a person for cutting him off. But she wouldn't stand silent.

"We did what we had to do."

"Yes, well. So am I. And as far as trusting Eric Gardner, he's already proven himself as good as his word on one account." Auldborne's jaw muscles pulsed.

"What's that?" Ellie asked.

"He gave me another shot at you." Auldborne paused then broke into a wicked smile. "Now, let's all go outside, shall we? I was beaten once on these docks by Blue. I intend to return the favor. In front of everyone."

When the five of them exited the museum, Ellie and Mazaryk first, with three guns at their backs, the crowd was whipped into a frenzy. A perimeter had been set while they were inside, patrolled by police and Tournament security officers, dressed in suits, who walked the ropes like bouncers. The front ranks of wonks frothed, cheered, and booed. They wore blue and grey, and many wore amber–colored headbands on foreheads and wrists in the German tradition. Several wonks tried to make a run toward them, but all were clotheslined by security. The lights were blinding, and the helicopters churned the water and kicked up the dust around them. Everything seemed to vibrate.

"Now!" Auldborne yelled, "Kneel! Kneel by the water. Both of you. This will be my aperitif before the German main course."

Mazaryk and Ellie refused to move. "If you're going to kill me," Ellie screamed, "just do it." Her back was to the water, her face to the crowd. She noticed Auldborne's gun was trembling, which she knew for a fact had never happened before. Auldborne was the surest shot there was. He had a surgeon's grip. She also noticed someone else, behind Auldborne. She singled him out because he was neither cheering nor booing. He was stock still, grinning like a scarecrow. He wore shorts and running shoes, and his feet were set a shoulder width apart. His hands were in the pockets of his cargo shorts, and he wore a T–shirt, too tight on him, of a variety sold at the souvenir stores around the country. It was blue and had the Tournament logo front a center and under that, the words *shoulda picked me!*

She knew immediately that she was looking at Eric Gardner.

When her eyes fell on him, his went as wide and round as golf balls. He waved slowly at her.

"Eddie," Ellie said, elbowing him, "it's him! There he is!"

But Eddie Mazaryk was turned around, looking out toward the water, where, in the distance, a bright light danced wildly. Closer and closer it came until Ellie could make out the high pitched whine of powerful engines. It was a speedboat, lit up like a Christmas tree in the colors of the German flag. It ripped through the waves, its wake jostling the boats it seemed to miss by mere feet. It was coming straight for them.

Ellie whipped her head back around and found Auldborne staring at her, his mouth set in a frown, his gun shaking. His eyes flicked toward the oncoming boat then back to her. Behind him, she saw Eric Gardner nodding.

"Do it," Gardner said. At first she could only read his lips. Then she heard him scream, "Do it, Alex!" The roar of the speedboat engine became far too loud, and Ellie knew it wasn't going to stop.

Several things happened at once. The first was that the speed-boat slammed into the dock between the museum entrance and where they stood. Ellie heard the first, eardrum–shattering instant of the explosion before everything became a muted buzz. She felt the heat of the engines blowing to pieces, and she saw her shadow flash over the crowd in a millisecond of searing white.

The second thing that happened was that Alex Auldborne let his gun fall to his lap and dropped his head down.

The third thing was that Eric Gardner broke through the line, untouched by security, his face livid and splotchy, beads of froth at the corners of his mouth. He tromped over to where Alex sat in his chair and picked Alex's gun up.

"God *dammit!*" he screamed, his face right next to Auldborne's ear. "All of this work and in the end, I have to do it myself. There was no better time. You had the crowd screaming for blood. You had the gun and the diodes. You thought the Germans were bearing down upon you. Ellie is *right there!* You were in the crucible, Alex, and you crumbled. I always knew you were only three tool talent. Just a lucky sonofabitch."

"*Thought* the Germans were screaming toward us?" Alex mumbled, hitching his head up. "You mean they weren't?"

"No, of course they weren't. You think they'd blow themselves up for you? They were never coming. That was my boat. Autodriver. Damned expensive too. The whole point of this was for you to shoot Ellie, and possibly Eddie, and you fucked it up."

Eric Gardner swung his head up like a bulldog and stared at Ellie. "You," he said in a low, guttural hiss.

"Hello Eric." Ellie realized she was standing alone. Eddie Mazaryk was on his back. A piece of the boat had struck him. His eyelids fluttered, but he was otherwise still. "'Shoulda picked me,'" Ellie said, reading his shirt. "But they didn't pick you, did they? They passed you over for John Northern. Is that what all this is about? You came in second, so you want to ruin the game for everyone else?"

Ellie could tell that she'd surprised him. The crowd around them had quieted, either in shock or because they wanted to hear what was being said, but either way, Ellie's voice could be heard loud and clear.

Gardner looked around, laughing loudly. "Why play the game when you can control it? Right?" He raised his voice. "They didn't pick me to fight, but they picked me for something else, something better, because I can read people. They came to me and said, 'You won't fight with them, but you will recruit them.'"

"And you were disappointed," Ellie said. "No matter how you spin it, you were behind the scenes when you wanted to be front and center. You don't strike me as a behind the scenes guy, Eric. You wanted my job, but they gave it to Northern."

Gardner seemed to be working words around in his mouth, his eyes impossibly wide and brimming with madness. Then he shrugged.

"You got me. Guess the jig is up. You figured me out. It's true. Northern was a four tool captain. And I..." He tapped Auldborne's gun briefly to his chest. "I humbly submit that I would have been a five tool player in my day. I know this because it is my fucking job to know. It is what I do."

"And what about me?" Ellie tried and failed to keep the strength in her voice.

"Two tool player. Guts and brains. And that's being generous. Two at best," Gardner said, without skipping a beat.

This was Ellie's chance to ask the question that had been tugging at her for years. The big unanswered riddle of her life that had come to define her insecurities, magnify her fears, and dampen her successes.

"Then why did you recruit me?"

"To fail, of course."

His words hit her with more force than any diode. They cut as deeply as Tom's death and raked over the raw wound in her heart left by Greer's absence. There it was. Greer was right when he said she was better off not knowing, but now it was too late. She'd been chosen to fail.

"I admit," the Gardner said, "that I'm kind of a bitter guy. I get that all the time. I'm a poor loser. It's something I'm trying to work on. When I found out that they'd passed me over and I had the chance to recruit the next captain, I chose the worst person I could possibly pass off to my peers without being laughed out of the room. That was you."

Ellie shook her head to ward off his voice. She stumbled to the ground a few feet from the water.

"Your victory at the Black House was a fluke, of course. Everyone knows that. You basically had four teams on your side. I couldn't possibly have accounted for that. You just happened to be the last standing, but still, I couldn't let that happen again. So I hatched an idea. I had the resources of the Tournament. I knew the people, the inner sanctum. Why not just… take it over?" He reached out and grabbed the air in front of him as he walked toward Ellie.

"I know every team inside and out. I picked the strongest and told them that if they followed me, they would win. I delivered. I will continue to deliver. See, you are the captain of one team. I am the captain of many, many teams. Among Northern, you, and me, you tell me who shines brightest in the end."

Ellie backed up against the water's edge.

"Go ahead and say it. I'm crazy, I've lost my mind. Yeah, that's what I knew you'd say, you and all of the original teams. You have this old–school chip on your shoulders. That's why I had to get rid

of you. None of you would get out of my way. You think you created the Tournament. The newer generation is much more malleable. They love my flowers."

In those last moments, Ellie's eyes saw past the Gardner, and
she saw ghosts again. This was a graveyard of sorts, after all, so it
was appropriate. She saw Tom floating through the crowd, silently
watching her, his blue eyes faded nearly to white but full of sadness
and understanding. She saw others who seemed out of place: her
mother and father covering their eyes, Ian watching her carefully,
weighing her transgression.

The Gardner stepped in front of her and cut all of them off.
"I told myself, if I ever got into this situation, I wouldn't run my
mouth, but I went and did it anyway." The Gardner sucked in a
huge breath. "Goodbye, Ellie. You were my greatest failure." He
raised Auldborne's revolver, and he shot Ellie right in the gut.

The wind left Ellie's lungs as if sucked from her mouth. She
crumpled and fell off the dock and into the water.

*

The Gardner watched Ellie splash then turned around and dropped
Auldborne's gun back in his lap. Auldborne's eyes were fixed on the
spot where had Ellie disappeared, and his frown hadn't left him.

"See?" the Gardner said. "Not that hard."

*

Ellie saw more ghosts. Floating to her left and right were Northern
and Hix but not in their bloated, dead aftermath. They floated next
to her peacefully, young and bright and whole, watching her with
small smiles that seemed to say, "*This damn water, it has claimed
us all,*" as if it were an inside joke. Only Ellie didn't want to be let

in on the joke. And if this was death, why did her stomach hurt so much? Every other player hit by a red diode died instantly. She didn't feel dead. She felt like she couldn't breathe and like she was going to throw up at the same time.

In fact, it felt an awful lot like Ellie had been shot in the gut with a regular old diode—like it was another bad day at the office. But she was sinking, nonetheless, and soon it wouldn't matter what she'd been shot with. She'd drown and end up like the ghosts circling her head. She reached for them with the last of her strength, grabbing water, and more water, and more water... and then a hand. The hand found hers, reached around and gripped her by the wrist, and pulled. Ellie surged up, through her ghosts, and her head broke through the water, and she saw Ian Finn, his legs planted firmly on the wooden dock, his face strained, as he gripped her with his other hand, his wounded hand. It closed around her arm with a crushing grip. He pulled her up and out of the water, and together, they collapsed in a heap. Ellie took in a sucking gasp.

*

Eric Gardner had watched Finn break free of the cordon, spin around the police and security, and race past both him and Auldborne to the water's edge. It didn't occur to him to stop the man. The deed was done, anyway. Let him pull a dead body from the water. It might serve him better to have his example laid out on the dock for the world to see, netted like a prize fish. But then Ellie moved. She groaned on the dock, coughing, and rolling over on her side with her hand clutching her gut.

Gardner clenched his teeth. He felt his face reddening, his heart pounding. He took off his baseball cap and threw it to the ground.

He balled up his fists, tromped over to Auldborne's chair, and screamed right in his face: "You didn't load the red diodes?"

*

Auldborne watched Ian pull Ellie from the water with a blank face, but his eyes betrayed him. If he could have, he would have reached for her himself. When she moved on the dock, he let out a breath of relief—a very small breath. His face remained blank as he watched the Gardner charge him, but his hands betrayed him. They clicked the chamber of his gun from round to round, slowly, methodically. Auldborne counted each click.

"That's a regular diode hit, Alex." Eric Gardner flailed his arm toward where Ellie lay on the dock. "You loaded regular diodes in your gun, you worthless excuse for a captain!"

"Not all of them," Alex said, his voice as cold and flat as a mountain lake.

"What are you talking about?" Gardner threw his hands up in exasperation.

"I said, not all of them are regular diodes. One of them is a good old–fashioned bullet."

Auldborne sighted the Gardner deftly, fired once, and blew the top of his head clean off. He fell backward, his hands and feet wide, his eyes still bulging, as though he'd taken a bad tumble skiing. The parched wood drank up his blood until it overflowed, and Auldborne's wheelchair cut two lines through the deep, viscous red as he passed the Gardner by on his way to where Ellie and Ian lay. They had seen everything, but Ian still stood and guarded Ellie, stepping between her and Auldborne.

Auldborne stopped his chair several feet from them and regarded them carefully. Here stood the man who was primarily responsible for his crippled condition, or so he'd thought for all of these years. He wasn't so sure anymore. The more he'd had a chance to think about it, and the more the Gardner had brought things in perspective for him, the more Auldborne wondered if he himself had at least as much to do with his own downfall as the couple in front of him. Exactly how much, he didn't yet know, but it was enough not to kill Ian Finn today.

From the ground, Ellie, still conscious, spoke. "You never planned to load the red diodes."

"Oh, I planned on it," Auldborne said. "But I changed my plans."

"How did you know he wouldn't shoot me with the real bullet?"

"I didn't." Auldborne smiled. "But again, I planned on him only using one shot."

"Why?" Ellie asked, at last. "Why did you stop him?"

"His way is no way to win. So I did what I had to do." Auldborne spun in his chair and glided back over toward Tate and Stoke, who seemed remarkably collected, as if things had progressed exactly how they knew they would. Auldborne paused next to where Eddie Mazaryk lay still. He threw his covering off and used his arms to hitch out his legs so that he could get a low purchase while still holding on to his chair. With his free hand, he felt at Mazaryk's neck for a pulse. He found one. Satisfied, he climbed his way back to a settled position and glided away.

This time, the crowd roared for him.

CHAPTER TWENTY

KEITH SNEDEKER'S ROUND table had turned on him. For the first time in his career, he was feeling very vulnerable in his corner of the ring. Dr. Eichler and Mr. Woo had both declined to appear that night, and Keith had the feeling that they might decline indefinitely. He pleaded with his producer to postpone the program.

"A man has just died," Keith told her, mopping his brow, mere minutes before air time. "Whether he was good or bad shouldn't matter. Don't you think it's a bit... *tacky* to go on air right now?"

"I see. So it wasn't tacky when Tom Elrey died. Or Ignazio Andizzi."

"Yes, but, this was a quite visible death. With all the blood and whatnot—"

"We're on in five, Keith. Sit down." She stared at him until he moved onto the stage, and in that stare Keith swore she could read his mind about how he'd wanted to keep her under his thumb. Had he said that out loud? His mind raced. His dinner of oysters and champagne, a celebration of sky-high ratings to come that suddenly seemed a bit premature, bubbled in his gut.

The ratings would be sky–high, all right. Keith just wasn't so sure he wanted the attention right now. *How strange*, he thought, *not to want attention*. He felt a rumble down below and popped his fourth antacid.

He popped a fifth as he entered the studio and found out who *had* shown up for the panel: Sarah Walcott, Frank Youngsmith, and Allen Lockton.

"Ah, yes, hello, all," he stammered, stepping slowly up on the stage, making his way to his seat. "Good to see you again." He was sweating profusely. His collar was already damp. He could feel it. Where was that damn makeup girl? There were usually three or four of them circling him, but now they were all on the other side of the table, tending to his three guests.

"Sweetheart," he addressed one, "would you be a dear?" He pointed at his neck. The girl stared at him. She turned back to Frank without a word. Snedeker cleared his throat.

"All right, then," he said, breathing through his nose. "When are we on?"

"One minute, you jackass," said the cameraman.

"Well now!" Keith said, mustering very little bluster. "Of all the… what is your name? You're fired."

The cameraman was silent. Keith turned to his producer. "What is his name?"

His producer was silent. The cameraman counted down, five, four, three, two… one was signaled with his middle finger. And they were live.

Keith wiped his upper lip. "Hello and welcome to *Tournament in the Round* where we, ah… where we…"

"Stay ahead of the players," Sarah said coolly.

"That's right!" Keith smoothed his tie. "That's what we do. I'm Keith Snedeker, the most trusted name in Tournament news"— Keith heard loud snickering off camera—"here with our three panelists, a bit of a light load today. With me are Sarah Walcott, Frank Youngsmith, and Allen Lockton. Glad to have you back, gentlemen."

Frank and Lock leaned in and stared at Keith, saying nothing.

"Yes. Well. Quite the revelatory night we've had! I don't need to tell any of you, dear viewers, what has just happened. It seems the whole world was watching as the three remaining original teams thwarted what many wonks around the world are now calling the most diabolical hostile takeover attempt that the Tournament has ever seen."

Snedeker stopped reading the teleprompter. "Diabolical? Isn't that a bit much?"

"No, Keith," Frank said.

"All right, then, we'll go with diabolical." Keith shuffled his notes. "A man calling himself the Gardner was behind the yellow roses after all, just as our two... esteemed panelists here... insisted not even two days ago. I admit I was far too hasty to dismiss." Snedeker pressed his hand flat to his chest and bowed his head deeply.

"As more details are unearthed—many coming straight from the mouths of the Pursers themselves—the full extent of the Gardner's agenda is being pieced together as we speak, and it is staggering in its scope. Promises of political power, wealth, and blood given to his chosen teams, taken from those he deemed unworthy, starting with the original Tournament teams."

Snedeker turned to the panel, his spectacles sliding down the bridge of his nose.

"Who could have seen this coming, ladies and gentlemen?"'

"We did, Keith. Remember?" Lock said.

"I do. Yes. Very perceptive. It appears that you've played yet another memorable part in yet another important chapter in the Tournament's history. Congratulations!"

The three stared at him.

"The good news is that this Eric Gardner lunatic was stopped. Think of what he could have done." Keith turned to the cameras. "More, after these messages."

The camera lights stayed red.

"More, after these messages," Keith said again.

His producer shook her head slowly. Keith heard a high-pitched scratching sound, like nails on a chalkboard. He winced, turned back to the panelists, and found Sarah Walcott slowly pushing a glittering yellow rose across the table toward him. It seemed to take an hour to reach even the middle of the table, where she let it rest in full view of the cameras.

"Care to explain this, Keith?" Sarah asked.

"That is the surprise that came out of the Countdown Box this cycle," Keith said softly, eying it as if it were a scorpion.

"Surprise to us, yes. Wasn't such a surprise to you though, was it, big guy?" Frank said.

"Specifically, Keith, I'd like to know why you kept this in

your vanity, front and center, from the day it appeared," Sarah asked.

"Well, it's quite beautiful," Keith said. "I was just going to admire it for a time, before giving it to charity, like we always do…" Keith felt light–headed. He took several huffing breaths and steadied himself on the table.

"I always wondered how it was that you got right of first question," Sarah said. "Out of nowhere, there's Keith. First all the time. Front row. Top billing. Very odd. I'm sure some of our competitors, who are no doubt watching tonight, also found it strange. So the three of us are going ask you again, Keith, before we take this godforsaken rose and pluck its jewels and melt it down to a puddle of platinum, sell it, and donate the proceeds to whatever charitable organization your competing networks collectively deem fit…" Sarah leaned in, clasping her hands demurely on the table. "How long. Have you been working. For Eric Gardner?"

Snedeker felt the weight of unseen eyes like the pressing of stones upon his chest. The cameras he'd mastered for so long, making them dance for him like lions at the whip, had turned on him. As they tracked toward him, their cold eyes conjured images in his mind of a spider about to dine. And speaking of dining, he really should have rethought that oyster and champagne dinner.

"How long?" Snedeker asked, his face green. "Long enough."

He lost his oysters all over the round table.

Epilogue

ALL OF A sudden, the world wanted to see much more of Ellie Willmore, Eddie Mazaryk, Alex Auldborne, and their teams.

The same wonks who had been subtly and not so subtly calling for their retirement were now rallying around the networks with campaigns to keep them fighting. The internet forums brimmed with stories of how the scrappy old guard had put the new kids in their place. Those who'd seen one of the original eight fight in person were elevated to a different level of fandom. Anyone who'd seen what happened at Chula Vista the second time around was counted among the most fortunate fans of all. Eric Gardner's final words to Ellie were turned against him: the top selling piece of Tournament paraphernalia quickly became a T-shirt design that read FAIL LIKE A CHAMPION in bright blue letters.

The wonks got together shortly after the events on the docks, convened for less than three days online, and came to the unanimous decision that what had happened would go down as a major event. They named the entire affair of that summer, from the death of Greer to the confrontation at Chula Vista, the Summer Crush.

The networks analyzed and over–analyzed every angle of the events of that summer and found all sorts of moral, strategic, and academic takeaways. But the one that stuck with the fans and with the new teams was this: respect those who came before you. The new teams took it to heart. For months afterward, many of them hung blue, black, and grey bandanas from their pockets and around their necks as a nod to that final stand. It was their first real education in the notion that the Tournament wasn't meant to serve them, that perhaps it was the other way around.

Ellie never succumbed to her stomach wound. Once Grey left the scene, the medics stepped in. They threw a sheet over Eric Gardner and split their crew between tending to Ellie and to Mazaryk. Ellie was loaded onto a stretcher and carried beyond the cordon to an open lot behind the crowd. Thousands of people ringed the space and watched as the medics, with Ian's help, loaded her into a helicopter. They held on to their hats and held their hair as the chopper took off on a straight line to UCSD Medical, where the Tournament had its own research wing. The doctors there were able to stop the bleeding before she dropped unconscious. They told her it was remarkable how long she'd held out. Ellie said it was because Ian had talked to her the entire time.

Eddie Mazaryk was hit by a jagged piece of bow on the right side of his body. Doctors would later say that the only thing that saved him was the fact that the chunk of material was so large it hit from his cheek to his knee, spreading out the force. Anything smaller would most likely have taken his head off. Tournament medics called for a second chopper to lift him out, but before it could land, Goran Brander and Ales Radomir appeared out of the crowd as if they stepped from the shadows. Brander's cane *thunked* heavily along the wood, and he stayed the medics with a look. Ales kneeled and carefully pushed his hands under his captain before lifting him smoothly into his arms. With Brander leading the way, they carried Mazaryk to a helicopter of their own that landed feet before them. They barely broke stride as they were lifted into the sky. Mazaryk was bruised from head to toe but otherwise unhurt.

The night of the Summer Crush would be Keith Snedeker's last night at USTN. The next evening, *Tournament in the Round* was renamed *Tournament Nightly with Sarah Walcott*. The transition was seamless. Ratings improved. As for Keith Snedeker, he was disgraced, but the fact remained that there was no actual crime in fighting for the right for first question. He moved to late–night cable. His show maintained a disturbing core of devoted fans. Sarah Walcott occasionally brought the most outlandish of them on as panelists on her own show to remind people of how things could have been.

The Summer Crush didn't end the Tournament cycle. In fact, many participant countries didn't even realize what was happening in Chula Vista. There were sixty–eight teams, after all. Those still in the running had better things to concern themselves with—namely, how they were going to win their next round. Team Grey did eventually fight Team Amber. The Germans tried to catch Auldborne's team unaware in London. They didn't succeed. Grey beat them handily. Stoke suffered a minor leg wound.

Auldborne's luck ran out in the fourth round when the

Jamaicans lured his team into an elaborate trap that involved miring his wheelchair in sand, locking Draden Tate's gun arm to a drain pipe, and trapping Christina Stoke in a taxi cab. Still, it was the best showing Grey'd had in over ten years. They were one round away from the final four. When they were revived in London, the English threw them a parade. Jamaica would go on to win the Tournament.

Cy forgave Ellie for her quiet departure the day of the fight, and Troya privately thanked her with an enormous hug. Ellie stayed with Cy and his family at the Cheyenne compound for another three months. She ate dinner with Cy, Troya, and Maddie every night. Cy brought Maddie's crib into their bedroom and gave Ellie the second bedroom. Ellie felt at peace there, but every now and then, Cy would walk to the kitchen to get a glass of water late at night and find Ellie sitting on the couch, keeping her mind busy. On the first day of the third month, Cy came out to get a glass of water late at night and found Ellie on the couch, but this time Ian Finn was with her. Cy said hello and smiled all the way back to his bedroom.

Two weeks later, on Halloween, when Blue held their annual Trick or Treat Safe Street for the Cheyenne kids, and after the candy had all run out, Troya told Ian and Ellie that she was pregnant. Cy smiled from the kitchen. When it was explained to Maddie, she cried. Then she laughed.

One day in mid–November, four bulldozers showed up at the Cheyenne compound. There was no forewarning, no press release, as they mowed down Cy's house and then Tom's, which had sat empty and haunting for almost half of a year. It shocked those fans who were outside the cordon that day to see how quickly everything was leveled. In a matter of hours, the Cheyenne compound was nothing but rubble. Neither Ellie nor Cy left any forwarding address.

The USA Tournament community was heartbroken. The same people who had been calling for Ellie's head mere months ago wept inconsolably at her quiet departure. Sarah Walcott spent many nights on *Tournament Tonight* talking the wonk community out of hysterics. "Did you think she would fight for you forever? Haven't they given enough?"

Three weeks after the Cheyenne compound was leveled, Sarah Walcott brought Frank Youngsmith and Allen Lockton back on the show. The set was entirely changed. Instead of Snedeker's round table with high-backed leather chairs, the three of them sat in comfortable loungers around a small wooden coffee table. After catching up, Sarah Walcott got down to business.

"What have you two been up to since the Summer Crush?"

"The mail never stops," Lock said.

"And have you delivered to… her?" Sarah's already polished persona cracked a bit, reverting back to the college girl. "Have you seen Ellie?"

"Yes," Frank said simply. "We have. And she gave us these." He reached into Lock's messenger's bag and withdrew three blue folders, tattered and worn at the edges, but still richly colored and reflective around the Tournament logo at their center. He set them down carefully on the table and spread them out like playing cards.

"Are those what I think they are?" Sarah asked.

"They're the commissioning folders that each of them received on the day they were brought into the Tournament. Ellie gave them to Lock and to me because she wants us to move on. All of us. It's time we started building a new team."

Sarah touched the top folder reverentially before turning to Frank. "Who will build it?"

Frank looked at Lock, who held up his hands.

"I'm just a courier, my friend," Lock said.

"Then I guess they chose you, Mr. Youngsmith," Sarah said.

Frank stared mutely at the folders for a full twenty seconds until Sarah cut to commercial break.

The next day, a package arrived at the Palo Alto Couriers' HQ addressed to *Mr. Frank Youngsmith.* In it were the keys to the administrator's office at Blue HQ. The return address read simply: RECRUITMENT. Frank shook his head and fumbled with the keys and questioned all of his abilities until Lock eventually just kicked him out and sent him next door.

"I'll be a quarter mile away, you big baby," Lock said. "Go figure out how to win the Tournament. No pressure."

Frank eventually opened up his new office and stepped inside, grinning like a schoolboy. The next day, he hired Brandt on a provisional basis. The first thing he said to him was, "I know where Ellie lives. If you screw with us again, I'll tell her where you live." Brandt wept with joy the moment he sat down behind his old desk outside the main office where Frank was already on the phones.

Eddie Mazaryk was true to his word. He recovered quickly from his bruising injury and then simply disappeared along with Brander and Ales. His last act as a Tournament captain was to hire Lock to pick up one final package. It proved to be Lock's most difficult assignment to date, and he left two cars, one motorcycle, one motor scooter, and one bicycle in various ditches and beside various roads before he finally reached his destination: an enormous linden tree in the quiet countryside many miles outside of St. Petersburg. There, he found a box. He picked it up and looked around. In the distance, he saw the glint of glasses, a flash of silver hair, and then the waving of a cane, but only for a second before all three blinked from view.

He carried the package to Moscow and delivered it to the center of Red Square, where he found a crowd of many thousands already waiting for him. He opened it in front of them and on camera as instructed. Inside, he found Black's three guns wrapped in the Russian flag. There was note. It read: *To the next three: Be good to her. We are watching.*

That left Team Grey as the only remaining member of the original eight still left in the Tournament, which, if rumors were to be believed, would be expanding to nearly one hundred teams in the near future. Alex Auldborne was quiet these days. The networks speculated that his newfound calm stemmed from the fact that he'd proven himself beyond what even a champion could do that night on the docks. Ellie had unmasked the Gardner, but Auldborne had put a stop to him.

Auldborne, Tate, and Stoke still resided at Auldborne's Hyde Park residence and were occasionally seen on the third–floor balcony, sipping drinks and laughing, and their country stood staunchly behind them. One day, years later, not long after rumors of a small, private wedding in Northern Ireland circled the Tournament networks, another rumor grew. Sanjay Paik, the head wonk for England, managed to stop Auldborne on the street. Auldborne allowed it, calming Tate and Stoke with a look.

Paik was breathless. "There's rumor that the Pursers have reached consensus. The draw is coming. Please..." And here he contemplated getting on his knees before thinking better of it, mostly because he knew Auldborne would be disgusted with him. "You're the last of the great teams. We all want to know if you'll be back. Please tell me you aren't retiring."

Auldborne stroked the worn leather of the holster built into his chair.

"Retire? I wouldn't dream of it."

About the Author

B. B. Griffith was born and raised in Denver, Colorado.

After graduating from Washington University in St. Louis with a degree in English and American literature, he wandered the world a bit before returning to Denver to set up shop with his wife.

For more information about the Tournament series of novels and to be notified of future releases by B.B. Griffith, join his mailing list online at

http://www.griffithpublishing.com/tournament/

Made in the USA
San Bernardino, CA
21 December 2015